the Midnight Beach

a novel by

TOM HEINAN

*This book is dedicated to my friend Flora,
who inspires me daily with her courage and tenacity.*

1

Ana paused for a moment to consider the footprints fading back into the sand behind her. Slowly the briny sea would flow up into her heels, then her toes, and saturate the prints, mixing the beach into her stride and feathering the traces of her journey. She turned back to face the wind as it tousled her hair with a chilly saline breath, the scent of kelp and sea-foam fresh upon her brow. The night sky above her was devoid of moon and stars, but the strand was nonetheless bathed in a selenitic blanket of silver light.

To her left, the ocean stretched out to the black edge of the horizon, waves cresting, crashing, and flowing back again against the fine-grain sand. To her right, dunes and scruffy tufts of grass rose up in defiance of the endless churn of the sea. Ahead of her, the dunes had made an inroad—a small but prominent cliff rising up over the surrounding beach and reaching out into the waves. Atop this gentle slope, there was a light, and Ana felt herself drawn toward its warm glow, a welcome beacon in the cold and tumultuous night.

As she approached and began to ascend the promontory, the source of this curious glow rose into view. To her surprise, the light she had seen was pouring from a lantern, itself attached to the top of a long wooden stave. The stave was held aloft by the hand of a monument—a curious amalgamation of dark brown burlap and gnarled, sea-worn driftwood. The shape before her stood tall, perhaps twice her own height, and cut the image of a man of curious proportions. The head comprised roughly one-third of the figure's total size, and the body seemed small and stocky in relation. Drawing ever closer, she looked up, searching for a face inside that ponderous hood, but was met instead by a tremendous skull, fashioned of driftwood, fringed with kelp and the pocks of wayward barnacles. Despite the macabre appearance, the expression was soft and attentive.

Now at the foot of this figure, Ana gazed up into its eye sockets, noting a curious blue-white glimmer—perhaps a reflection of the sea-tinged glow around her.

"Who are you?" she said aloud.

"Doro." The voice was deep and resonant, but calm.

Ana gasped in surprise. Had this pile of burlap and driftwood just spoken? Her eyes darted up and down the empty shoreline. As far as she could tell, she was alone.

The statue spoke again. "Who are *you*?"

Creeping forward, she squinted into the wind-worn cowl, studying the lines of the figure's empty eye sockets and the rows of wooden teeth. "My name is Ana," she said at last.

"Nice to meet you, Ana." Doro lifted up his staff, the lantern at the top clanking softly as he gestured toward the shoreline. "Welcome to the Midnight Beach."

He turned into the wind and took a few broad steps forward to the tip of the bluff. Cautiously Ana crept up and took a place by his side.

After a few moments punctuated only by the pulse of the ocean breeze, Doro spoke. "Is something wrong?"

Ana looked up again at the curious driftwood man. "I'm sorry. I guess I've never met someone quite like you before."

Doro's wooden visage was ostensibly motionless, but nonetheless, she thought she could detect a faint smile.

"I've met many young men and women in my time," he said.

"Do a lot of people come here?"

"Many, yes." Doro continued to gaze out into the vast inky darkness beyond the churning waves. "Though you are the first in quite some time."

Ana frowned, inhaling sharply as she brought her sleeve to her nose and blinked the mist out of her eyes.

"Why have you chosen to come here?" There was no judgment in his voice.

"I'm looking for someone."

"A friend?" he asked. "Or a loved one?"

Ana furrowed her brow, folding her arms across her chest in defense against the biting gusts. "Both, I guess." Her voice trembled.

"Many come to the Midnight Beach in hopes of finding things they have lost. Some come to lose the things they've found. You, I think, may be somewhere in the middle."

Ana opened her mouth to reply, but the sea wind swallowed her voice.

Slowly Doro turned to face her, then continued past her and down off the hill. He made his way along the beach, Ana following a few feet behind.

"The person I'm looking for … I thought maybe she'd have come through here before me."

As Doro continued in contemplative silence, Ana looked down to discover they were following an increasingly well-defined path, up through the dunes and away from the swelling and crashing water.

"Her name is Amber. She has dirty-blond hair and glasses—average height. She wears a lot of retro T-shirts. She told me a couple of days ago she might be headed this way … I haven't heard from her since then."

Gradually the beach began to give way to rockier terrain, and Doro picked his way along the shore with his stave, lantern clanking back and forth as he maneuvered around the debris.

"How long have you been out here?" asked Ana.

"Many years. Perhaps more now than I can remember. But I like the solitude of the beach. Sometimes the squalls keep me away from the shoreline, but most nights, the sea is calm enough."

As sheer rocks rose up to enclose their path on either side, she approached Doro once more and turned her gaze to his lumbering skull. "And you haven't seen anyone else out here recently?"

Their path through the rocky cliffside opened out into a small outcropping. A low wall stood here, fashioned of cobble and weathered by the elements. It protected the opening of a sea cave. An occasional booming gust broke forth from the entrance, suggesting a connection to the ocean down below.

Doro turned and gazed down at Ana. She detected a hint of sadness in his guise.

"I do not think I have seen your friend Amber," said Doro. "But it is possible she did not come up this way on the beach."

Ana stood silently. The wind whistled through the rocks in quiet harmonies as she hugged her arms to her chest, fighting back a roiling shiver.

Doro stretched out his arm once again, the lamp atop his stave casting a warm glow into the mouth of the grotto. "Welcome to my home. You may stay as long as you like."

*　*　*

Beyond the unassuming entrance, the cave opened up into a cathedral of warm light. As the two made their way down into the cavern, Ana looked up to find a constellation of lanterns, each crafted from panes of sea glass in vivid blues and greens, bound together with wrought iron. Each lamp hung down on sturdy rope, affixed to a stalactite high above, and shifted back and forth in the breeze. The light bounced off the slick cave walls and glittered through the midnight air.

In the heart of this ancient cavern were arranged a number of simple furnishings—a dresser of drawers, a desk, a large bed, and various tables and chairs, all in immaculate condition. As Ana wandered into the midst of this collection, she began to appreciate the size of these trappings. They were clearly fashioned with Doro's stature in mind—the surfaces of the tables were barely visible from Ana's vantage point, and the chairs looked roughly table height.

"Come." Doro motioned over to a round table at the side of the room. It had only one chair, but it was much more suitably sized for an average person. "Let us share some tea."

Ana sat down in the wooden chair while Doro made his way to the side of the cavern. Carved into the rock wall was a basin stocked with coals. The embers were smoldering with radiant heat. Above this basin was a small hook. Doro reached up to a graven shelf and pulled down a kettle and some jars of herbs. Carefully he placed the herbs in the kettle and set it on the hook above the fire. He then produced two cups from his cloak—a larger clay mug for himself, and a smaller cup for Ana.

Soon steam began to rise from the kettle and float up into a chimney far above in the ceiling of the cavern. He pulled the kettle off its mooring and brought it over to the table. He poured the tea, first for Ana, then for himself. After setting the kettle down on the table, he bent his knees and lowered himself to sit cross-legged on the ground. For the first time, his head was more or less at eye level with Ana, and he gazed at her intently.

Ana looked into his deep and impenetrable eye sockets. The tea was warm and rejuvenating, tasting of rosemary and sage. She took a few pensive sips and cleared her throat.

"Thank you for inviting me into your home," she whispered.

"All are welcome," said Doro. He brought the mug to his teeth and seemed to savor for a moment the aroma of herb and steam. His tone changed, warmed. "Tell me about Amber."

Ana looked down into her cup. "I've known her since we were kids. We met in preschool. It was on Bainbridge Island. We were friends all the way through high school, but we ended up going to different colleges. After graduation, I came back to Seattle for a job, and I ran into her at a Starbucks. She was working there as a barista."

The lights in the cavern shimmered and swung with the pulse of the underground sea.

"At first we just hung out after work. I think our first date was a trip to go see *Rocky Horror*. She told me she was headed this way. I guess I thought she'd be waiting here." Ana smiled, but her eyes were wet.

"Perhaps she is," said Doro. "There are many ways to get here, depending on your preferred mode of transportation. To be honest, travel by sea is rare these days."

Doro put his mug down and placed a skeletal wooden hand on the ground. He pushed and lifted himself up to full height, retrieving his staff from its resting place against the cavern wall.

"Tomorrow we can set out for Istabar. But tonight, let us rest."

He crossed the room to a small couch made up with a few sheepskin blankets and a pillow. Ana stood and followed. She sat on the makeshift bed and instantly felt the weight of sleep upon her brow.

"You think Amber is in Istabar?"

"I do not know," said Doro. "But if you seek to find someone who has knowledge of her whereabouts, that is the first place I would look." He turned and made his way to a small opening in the opposite wall. Stairs led down to a deeper part of the cave. He stood on the precipice and looked back at Ana. "I admire your dedication," he said softly, then turned back and started down.

That night, the muted rolling of the ocean waves brought little comfort to Ana's sheepskin bed.

2

The road to Istabar was longer than Ana had anticipated. For several hours, she and Doro had been walking through the valleys between the dunes, where the sand was packed more tightly and progress was more easily made. The rumble of the ocean had long since given way to the muted hiss of sand skittering down from higher perches, dancing in the vagaries of softer winds.

They had shared the road so far in silence, broken only by the occasional chittering of native scarabs and other sparse fauna.

As the monotony settled in, Ana spoke. "What is Istabar like?"

"It is a city," said Doro, "grand in scale and opulent in affectation. It was built many years ago as a center of trade and today is home to individuals from all walks of life."

"And you think Amber might be there?"

"I do not know. But if she is not there now, she may have passed through recently."

"What's it like there?"

Doro thought for a moment. "Loud."

Ana furrowed her brow.

"The city itself is a great hub of activity, but we will need to focus our efforts if we are to find any useful information. I suspect we should start with the Weavers—they spend a great deal of time keeping tabs on the comings and goings of Istabar's denizens. No visitor goes unnoticed."

Ana slowed to a snail's pace, then stopped, and Doro turned to meet her gaze.

"I can't ask you to help me," she said. "I mean, even more than you already have."

"You can," said Doro. "It would be my pleasure. In fact, my privilege." He stretched out a bony wooden hand and gestured onward. "The city lies yet many leagues from here. We should not tarry long."

*　　*　　*

The path gradually became a well-worn dirt road. The dunes gave way to low scrubland, and small bushes dotted the landscape. Rolling hills covered in a golden blanket of tall grass slowly sprouted trees and covered the terrain in a thin layer of fine needles and mossy stones. The ocean was now a distant memory, but the air was no less fresh, enriched by the piney swell of higher elevation.

As they traveled up through the hills, the titter of birds and rustle of creatures in the now-plentiful underbrush punctuated an otherwise muted rumbling from nearby wandering creeks. Soon there was another noise, filtering through the trees, the distinct notes of conversation too far afield to be understood, but nonetheless clearly boisterous and lively.

As Ana and Doro rounded a corner, they met with a fork in the road. Parked at that fork was a sort of caravan—wagons and carts of various sizes and shapes, some covered, some not, some laden with barrels and boxes, others empty. A few men and women were arrayed about the carts, transferring goods from one area to another. At the head of the halted procession stood a diminutive creature in a purple-and-blue robe, directing much of the activity. He spoke in a high-pitched, raspy voice with a curious lilt, jovial but focused.

"Mmm, yes. That one there, take it back, and put it with the other dry goods. The mead, put it in the covered wagon—it will spoil in the sun."

As Ana approached, she saw not boots but paws, and two furry ears poking out of the creature's hood. Indeed, it seemed to be some sort of cat, standing on its two hind legs and orchestrating the process of moving cargo out of a broken cart.

"Those too, bring—ah, hello there!" He stepped forward and extended a paw from his intricately patterned robe. Ana held out her hand, and the cat grabbed it between his paws and shook it officiously.

"Hello," she said in disbelief.

"And your name is …?" asked the cat, with a curious look in his eyes.

"Oh, I'm sorry. It's Ana."

"Ana, yes, hmm," he said, gliding up and down with melodic intonation. "Well met. Well met indeed. You speak now with Ras Dashen."

"It's a pleasure to meet you, Ras Dashen," she said, still struck with bewilderment. Ana then turned her gaze to her traveling companion, who seemed not the least bit surprised to encounter a talking animal. "This is my friend Doro."

Ras Dashen stepped forward and bowed deeply. "Ras Dashen is pleased to make your acquaintance, sea watcher."

"Likewise," said Doro with a slight but respectful bow.

As Ana cast her eyes around the clearing, she realized for the first time that many members of this caravan were not human at all. Among the men and women of this convoy were bipedal animals of various kinds—cats, goats, and even a few cows. Here, too, were several men and women of diminutive stature, perhaps three or four feet tall, moving boxes around and fretting about the broken cart.

Doro noticed Ana's bemused expression. "Dwarves," he said. "A rare sight on the road up from Harveston these days."

Turning back to Ras Dashen, he addressed the feline once more. "What has transpired here with your caravan?"

Ras Dashen frowned. "This road is littered with rocks. We have come upon a stone that has broken a wheel on our lead wagon. In all his years, Ras Dashen has never had such bad luck with the coastal road."

Indeed, one of the two large wheels of the cart seemed to have broken apart atop a sizable chunk of granite. Several wooden spokes lay broken on the ground next to the ruptured wheel.

Ras Dashen gestured to the ruined cart. "It saddens me that we must leave it here, but the greater tragedy will be our spoiled goods if we can't get them to Istabar quickly. On top of that, we don't have enough room in the other carts to distribute the load."

"You're going to Istabar?" asked Ana. "We're headed there too … Maybe we can help."

At this, Ras Dashen's ears perked up. "Mmm, perhaps … perhaps you can. Help would be very much appreciated. Ras Dashen would be in your debt!"

Ana walked over to the cart and tied several bags of grain together. From the front, she salvaged some leather scraps. Tying them together, she fashioned a simple harness that enabled her to carry the grain and various other loose accoutrements as a makeshift backpack.

Doro bent down and gathered the remainder of the supplies, slinging them into two large canvas sheets and tying the bundles to both ends of his wooden stave. Then he hefted the stave across his shoulders. With this additional carrying capacity, Doro and Ana were able to make up for the loss of the cart, and the caravan was once again mobile.

"Excellent, excellent!" said Ras Dashen. He took up his place at the head of the party and hopped up the road. "This way to Istabar, friends!"

And so they set off, moving among the trees with renewed speed and purpose.

As the group continued toward their destination, Ana walked up next to Ras Dashen.

"Why are you going to Istabar with all these goods?" she asked.

"Ras Dashen will sell these goods at the bazaar. We collect from the Farmers and bring materials to market in return for a share of the profits. There is much food this time, and much drink. But there is also wool for the Weavers and steel for the Anvil. I think it will fetch a handsome price, yes, hmm. Thanks to you and your large friend for sharing the load! Ras Dashen does not know what he would have done without your assistance. A much less profitable journey, to be sure."

"Well, we're happy to help, and to be honest, I'm grateful for the company."

"What business do *you* have in Istabar?" asked Ras Dashen.

"I'm looking for a friend of mine. Doro thinks she may have come up this way from the Midnight Beach."

"Mmm ... and what does this friend of yours look like, hmm?"

"Well, she's got dirty-blond hair, medium height ... thin, I suppose."

Ras Dashen's furry brow contorted as he cast his gaze upward in contemplation. "Ras Dashen has not seen such a person in recent days," he said at last, "but he has not been in Istabar for over a month. Certainly, when we arrive, Ras Dashen will keep an eye out. If your friend is in Istabar, Ras Dashen is sure he can find her."

"Really?" For the first time in a long time, Ana felt hopeful that her quarry might not be so far off after all. "I hope so, Ras Dashen."

3

As the caravan rolled out of a dense pine thicket and into a clearing, Ana was surprised to see how much altitude they'd gained. Before them was a broad grassy valley, giving a wide berth to a large river flowing through the middle. On either side, the walls of the valley rose up to great peaks. Nestled in the heart of this valley and perched just above an enormous waterfall was a huge city, its bone-white ramparts glowing in the sunlight. It seemed to have been built around a great eruption of stone—a dramatic moraine, perhaps left over from some grand glacial flow in ages long past. Bold monuments, aqueducts, and buildings of all shapes and sizes scaled the jagged cliffs. In the center, a prodigiously tall tower reached up into the heavens.

"That," said Doro, "is Istabar."

As the caravan drew closer, Ana could see that the entire city was encircled by an enormous wall. It seemed at once ancient and impossibly advanced in construction. The surface was fashioned of smooth white stone—no pock or blemish could be seen for all the time these imposing ramparts must have spent in silent sentry over the surrounding valley slopes. Only great spires of ivy here and there, creeping far up the vertical surface, testified to the advanced age of this grand edifice.

Before them, at the terminus of the road, there was a huge gate carved into the wall. Five banners hung overhead. Each was a work of art in itself: a golden anvil upon a field of crimson; a white-and-sky-blue aegis; a plow emblazoned over a field of green flocking; a beautiful shimmering pattern of deep pinks, purples, and blues weaving into one another under an intricate needle and thread; and a large, ornate letter *D* stitched in gold over a black-and-orange sunburst.

Doro strode forward and stopped before the giant gate. The top of the wall towered many dozens of feet above even his formidable stature. He slung the makeshift yoke off his mighty shoulders and deposited his cargo on the ground. Stave now in hand, he rapped it several times against the smooth stone, lantern clanking back and forth loudly, and then stepped back, casting his gaze up to the ramparts in silent expectation.

A moment later, a furry muzzle peeked over the wall and called down in a gruff voice. "Yes?"

Ras Dashen stepped forward and bowed deeply. "Your humble servant Ras Dashen has returned from the fields of Cowling with many goods. Kindly let him pass through these hallowed gates, that he may enrich this great city with his wares."

"I recognize *you*, Ras. Who are these other travelers?"

Doro opened his mouth as if to speak but was cut off by Ana's shout. "My name is Ana. I'm from Seattle, and I'm looking for someone. I think she may have come to Istabar, so I've come to look for her."

"I am here to help," said Doro.

"These travelers are friends of Ras Dashen—they have aided him in his time of need, and thus he is duty bound to see to their safe passage into the city."

"Hmph. Very well. Check your friends in at the Registarium, and know that you are responsible for their behavior." With that, the guard departed from the wall.

A few moments later, a great rumbling sound preceded the scraping grind of stone as the gates slowly parted. Doro took up his cargo, and the caravan proceeded into the city. As the last cart rattled through the archway, the doors began their slow migration back to a closed position.

Traveling through the interior of the entryway, Ana was struck again by the beautiful, minimal simplicity of the architecture. The buildings were all fashioned from the same sort of sun-bleached white stone—whether impeccable masonry or just hewn out of solid rock, she couldn't tell, but the craftsmanship was astounding. Down from the windows and rooftop decks of the various towers and buildings inside the walls hung colorful banners depicting the various sigils of the guilds of Istabar.

It was then that Ana noticed the guards on either side of the promenade. They were dogs of various shapes and sizes, each wielding a large shield and a polearm. They wore helms and cloaks but were otherwise free from restrictive armor. They each stood on their two hind legs, like Ras Dashen, and kept watch at regular intervals along the walkway from the entry gate to a central courtyard. Along the walls of the buildings on either side, Ana noted a number of multitiered aqueducts pouring shimmering blue water into one another, feeding homes and businesses, turning small waterwheels, and cascading into small pools along the street. There they ran into small channels in the road and flowed into a central area in the courtyard—a pool in which was planted a beautiful tree with rainbow-colored leaves. Its roots were a fine lattice that grew directly out of the pool of crystal blue water at its base.

As the caravan reached this courtyard, the bustling traffic of the city came into full view. Men, women, children, dogs, cats, and all manner of curiously dressed entities mixed about in the streets and alleyways of this glittering jewel of commerce. Along the arcing streets and corridors were stationed various stalls with a variety of goods and services on offer.

Just to the left of the entrance to this courtyard was a small window, a sign hanging above clearly labeled

"Registarium of Istabar." Ras Dashen had wandered over with his waybill and was tallying the numbers back and forth with a goatlike fellow on the other side. Ras Dashen's retinue, meanwhile, had begun to unload their carts and set up a tent on the far side of the courtyard, in what appeared to be their usual location. Doro was assisting them, his size a particular asset in this endeavor.

As Ana scanned across the throngs of people crowding the streets, she saw for a moment a flash of blond hair as it disappeared down an alleyway. Immediately she took off running down the street, dodging and hopping around the various denizens and visitors of Istabar. She rounded a corner, ducked into the alley, and was at once confronted with a maze of streets, converging and diverging in between an incomprehensible mess of structures. She continued to run down the alley, stopping to look down each pathway on the left and right as she passed, until at last she came to an intersection at which forward progress ended with a steep, mossy cliff face. She gazed up from here to see only the enormous tower that dominated the center of the city. Defeated, she turned around and began to walk back to the bustle and noise of the bazaar.

As she passed the entrance to one of the side routes, however, a voice spoke out of the shaded gloom between the buildings. "You look a little lost."

Startled, Ana turned around to face the source of the observation. There was an older woman there, blond of hair, in pauper's garb, with a messenger bag slung across her shoulder.

"Oh, thank you, but no—I'm just on my way back to the market," said Ana.

"Best keep your wits about you in the alleys, Ana. Not everyone here is as friendly as Ras Dashen."

"How do you know my name? Are you a friend of Ras Dashen?"

"Everyone's a friend of Ras Dashen when it suits him. But take my advice: don't be so quick to trust in the kindness of strangers."

Ana raised an eyebrow. "So why should I trust you?"

The woman reached into her bag and produced a small pin. It seemed to be a garment clasp, adorned with a needle and thread. "Take this," she said, "and keep it close."

"What is it?"

"Just please hang on to this. For me—as a favor."

Ana hesitated, then reached out and accepted the pin. She turned it over in her hands, examining its intricate construction. After a moment, she looked up, but the strange woman had disappeared back into the shadows amid Istabar's looming infrastructure.

A shred of Ana's unconscious mind urged pursuit, but she instead pocketed the pin and turned back to the street, following it out again to the main thoroughfare and the courtyard, where Doro had now completed the effort of tent construction.

"I just met the most curious woman, Doro," said Ana.

"Istabar is full of curious people," said Doro. "Some too curious for their own good."

At that moment, Ras Dashen appeared, having apparently concluded his extensive business at the Registarium.

"Now then," he began, "Ras Dashen must spend the rest of the afternoon setting up the display. Perhaps you would like to assist."

"Normally, I would love to," said Ana, "but I fear that every moment I spend here, Amber gets farther away."

Ras Dashen bowed deeply. "Of course, of course." He began to turn back to the tent, then stopped and looked up at Ana, squinting in the midday sun. "Perhaps Ras Dashen can be of assistance to you now. The Registarium did not have record of a traveler named Amber visiting in the recent past." Ana frowned. "Despite this, Ras Dashen thinks it is best to speak with the Weavers. Not every traveler is registered, despite the council's best efforts. But if she is in this city somewhere, the Weavers will know about it."

"But how do I talk to the Weavers?"

"Normally, access to the lord and lady is tightly controlled—but Ras Dashen knows a few tricks." Reaching into a small chest nearby, Ras Dashen produced a tightly wrapped bolt of bluish-purple fabric, its delicate patterns flashing in the light.

"Take this to the Weavers' Guild as a show of good faith," he said, handing the parcel to Ana. "It never hurts to grease the wheels a bit if you are looking for information."

"Oh my," said Ana, marveling at the vivid hues that danced across the fabric's surface. "Thank you, Ras Dashen, but I can't take this from you."

"Nonsense. You helped Ras Dashen with his problem; now Ras Dashen will help you with yours," he said with a smile. Bowing deeply once again, he turned and began to make his way over to his compatriots, who had begun to unpack the rest of the caravan's goods in the welcome shade of their market tent.

Ana cradled the fabric in her arms and looked up at Doro. "Do you know where the Weavers' Guild is?"

"Follow me."

4

Several levels up from the courtyard, in the northern part of the city, a great guildhall sat in opulent simplicity. The exterior cut the figure of an enormous loom, and each strand stretched across its exterior was more brilliant and colorful than the last. Underneath this exquisite canopy were market stalls, entertainers, and patrons of all kinds.

Doro ducked under the facade and climbed up the steps behind Ana.

Inside, an open atrium revealed floor upon floor of weavers, spinners, knitters, and all manner of cloth craftspeople. An elevator in the center of the atrium rang sonorously, and out stepped a man with a bald head, a monocle, and a dazzling rainbow cloak.

He strode past Ana and Doro with an air of purpose, then stopped and spun around to take in the sight of the large skeletal driftwood man and his traveling companion.

"My word, Doro. What on earth happened to that cloak? It seems as though you've run it ragged. If you like, we can at least patch it up for you while you're here."

"Very kind of you to offer, Cornelius, but there will be no need for that today. In fact, perhaps it is we who may be of service to you."

Ana stepped forward and presented the bolt of cloth.

Taking it in hand, Cornelius worked it over, gazing into its dazzling folds and pinching the ethereal weave between his fingers. "Good heavens! Where did you find such a thing?" he asked at last.

"Consider it a gift," said Ana, not having thought to come prepared with a plausible backstory.

Cornelius was astounded at this. "But this is Sirens' Silk. One does not simply part with a gift such as this. If you truly wish to bequeath it to the Weavers' Guild, you should do so in person to Lord Various." He thought for a moment, weighing the threat of imposition against the gravity of the gesture. "Come with me."

*　　*　　*

The elevator slowed to a stop on the top floor, and its crystal-glass doors slid silently open. The trio walked out into an expansive receiving room, circular in shape. Couches upholstered in lustrous purple velvet lined the walls, and a grand chandelier, a kinetic mobile of colorful crystals, floated above. In the ceiling, a panel of glass let in the bright sunlight, which splashed the chandelier's colors around the immaculate white walls of the chamber. On the opposite side of the room was an opening into an office lined with floor-to-ceiling windows that afforded a breathtaking view of the pale stone maze of central Istabar and the grand tower rising up at its center.

In the center of the office was an opulent wood-and-glass desk, at which was seated a slender man with long, thin platinum hair and ice-blue eyes. His garments were unlike anything Ana had ever seen: an immaculately well-fitted but flowing jacket of sky blue and deep violet, with shimmering silver accents on the shoulders and the cuffs; slacks of matching purple with blue pinstripes; and an elbow-length crocheted cape that fell delicately about his shoulders and shifted in color as he moved his arm to scrawl in the sizable ledger before him. He looked up as he placed his pen into an ornamental inkwell stand and rose to his feet gracefully, stepping around the desk with arms wide open in a welcoming gesture.

"Ah, Ana, please do come in. I have been awaiting your arrival with bated breath!"

Cornelius and Ana stepped into Various's office, and Doro trailed behind, ducking down so as not to upset the delicate chandelier above.

"Cornelius tells me you've brought something to this humble house as a gift. May I see it?"

Ana produced the Sirens' Silk. Much like the cloak around Various's shoulders, it shifted in color as it moved through space, and brought a certain warmth and glow to every surface upon which it settled. She placed the parcel upon the desk and stepped back.

"My lord, I bring you a bolt of precious cloth in the hope that I might ask you for a favor in return."

Various gasped, transfixed by the fabric before him. He reached out reflexively with his hand and then stopped, looking up at Ana in reverence. "May I?"

Ana nodded, and he took up the cloth and brushed it slowly with his hands. "This is indeed the legendary Sirens' Silk. I do not know how to accept such a gift." He stared into the folds of the fabric for a short moment and then shook his head as if trying to wake from a hypnotic trance. "Forgive me. In my haste, I have entirely neglected to properly introduce myself. I am Lord Various Quinn, steward of the Weavers' Guild and petitioner to the council on behalf of the craftspeople of Istabar. But please, call me Various."

Ana, unsure of the social customs in Istabar, attempted a sort of awkward curtsy and replied, "Nice to meet you. I'm Ana. But I suppose you already knew that."

"Yes. My apologies for the presumption, but of course, the Weavers' Guild pays a great deal of attention to the comings and goings of the city. Enough attention, at any rate, to notice when individuals slip in without informing the Registarium of their arrival." He gestured for Ana to have a seat in a delicate-looking chair across from him as he returned to his place behind the desk. As he sat down, he looked up at Doro. "Apologies, old friend. I'm afraid I still haven't gotten around to procuring any appropriately sized furniture for a gentleman of your stature."

"None needed," said Doro, bending down to sit cross-legged on the immaculate pinewood floor.

"I understand you're looking for someone," said Various, "and it is my sincere hope that I can be of some assistance in this regard."

"Yes. Her name is Amber. She's medium height, brownish-blond hair, wears glasses but often forgets them …"

"Indeed. Several weeks ago, a young woman matching that description was spotted passing through the Westward Gate—the very same one you arrived through earlier today. Normally unremarkable, except that the Registarium does not have record of her entry."

Ana leaned forward and placed her hand on the desk, eager for even the barest credible lead, then slumped back with a frown. "But … she's only been gone a few days."

Various shrugged. "Perhaps this was not her first trip to Istabar. Nevertheless, with a bit more work, we may be able to uncover her current whereabouts." Various cast his gaze again upon the shimmering fabric on his desk. "The Weavers' Guild has many priorities, of course, and we cannot divert resources en masse from the safety and security of Istabar's merchants, but for such a generous gift … there are a few favors I am more than willing to call in." He smiled, then closed the ledger on his desk and handed it to Cornelius with a nod. Cornelius took the book in hand and departed with some haste.

Leaning forward across the desk, Various took Ana's hand in his and placed his other hand atop it. "I promise to do what I can to find Amber, but it will take some time. In the meanwhile, the Anvil are mounting an operatic re-telling of a very old story, and tonight is opening night. I would be honored if you and Doro would join me this evening."

Ana hesitated, looking down at her hand now gently but firmly ensconced in Various's grasp. "I would like that," she said at last.

5

The blanched and innumerable facades of Istabar glowed a fierce orange as the sun set over the valley. The great wall encircling the city cast a long shadow that enveloped the ground-level streets from west to east. Strings of light bulbs began to spring to life and bathe the alleyways in pale blues and greens. Higher up near the center of the city, an enormous opera house sat in the deepening shadow of the central spire. Its stone exterior was embellished with a rich tableau in bas-relief: dogs and cats armored and locked in mortal struggle, men and women entangled in the throes of passion, vivid landscapes depicting a layered cosmology, suns and stars, planets, gods and demons, and the ever-present language of music.

As Ana was marveling at the artistry, she realized suddenly that for the first time since her arrival on the beach, she was alone. Of course, the streets thrummed with passersby, and patrons were shuffling by the hundreds into the immense archways delineating the entrance to the opera, but tonight she was to venture inside unaccompanied. "I do not care for the opera," Doro had told her earlier. "People get upset when I sit in front of them. And in any case, I have an appointment this evening with Carver Olen, councillor of the Anvil. Enjoy the show, but do not let your guard down."

It seemed a silly thing, to have to steel oneself for an evening of leisure, but Ana was a stranger in this city, and she had a feeling that all in Istabar was not precisely what it seemed.

She ascended the exterior steps and crossed the threshold into the building. The interior of the opera house was even more striking than its exterior. Walking up to the box office, she noted the ornate and deeply traditional decor: wood-and-velvet seats, a flourish of elaborate molding on the walls, decorative colonnades, and all manner of intricate detailing that seemed to fly in the face of the city's otherwise minimal aesthetic.

"Good evening, miss." The voice came from a large, barrel-chested black dog behind the window of the box office. He sported a bluish-grey cloak, upon which was pinned a name tag that identified him as the theater's general manager. His jowls turned up toward the white bristles fringing his muzzle as he smiled.

"Good evening," said Ana. "I was told by Lord Various to collect my ticket here."

"Ah," said the dog, "you must be Ana. Here's your ticket. The Weavers' Guild box is just up the stairs to your left. Go all the way down the hall, and take the last right."

Ana nodded as she took the ticket and made her way up to the balcony level. After crossing the hallway into a box beside the stage's gilded proscenium, she took her place in an ornate chair, one of three set up for the Weavers' Guild this evening.

As the orchestra section filled up below, she eyed the crowd like a hawk. There were so many people here, and most of the women were wearing some form of fascinator or other head-obscuring device. Specks of blond hair flitted in and out of her vision, but none that betrayed the image of her quarry. So rapt was she at the growing wave of patrons that she did not notice the door open behind her.

"Good evening, my dear." The voice behind her was soft and mellifluous, and she knew it at once to be that of Lord Various, though she started in surprise just the same. "My apologies. I did not intend to startle you," he said, smiling.

"May I introduce you to my counterpart?" Through the door behind him stepped a woman. Despite her ravishing evening gown, Ana recognized her at once: it was the woman from the alley. She smiled at the sudden realization writ plainly over Ana's face. "Lady Sundry. Sundry, this is my dear friend Ana."

Sundry executed a deep curtsy and crossed in front of Various to take a seat next to Ana. "It's a pleasure to make your acquaintance," she said. "Various has told me so much about you."

Ana swallowed hard and fingered the pin in her pocket.

Sundry continued. "He showed me the cloth you brought to the guild this afternoon—truly an impeccable specimen. I'm curious how you came by such a rare commodity."

"It was gifted to me," said Ana, "and since I have no skill in tailoring, I thought it best to gift it on to you. Surely you will make much better use of it than I would."

"We will certainly endeavor to use it wisely," she said.

As Various took his seat beside her, the lights dimmed, and a solitary A note rang out from an oboe far below. Gradually the other instruments joined in, tuning up and down to center on harmonious agreement. A moment of silence fell on the theater, and then the orchestra roared into motion, painting an acoustic vision of dazzling highs and terrible lows as the overture washed over the audience.

Under cover of the cacophony below, Sundry leaned over to whisper in Ana's ear. "Do remember what I told you… 'gifts' do not exist in Istabar—only payment in advance."

As the music reached a fever pitch, the curtains parted to reveal a man and a woman standing in a garden. The man was draped in a flowing yellow cloak, with a large hood obscuring his face. Across from him stood a woman in plain dress, gazing out into the audience as she began her song. It was in a language Ana didn't understand, but it sounded familiar—Italian, perhaps, or Latin? The woman seemed not to notice the peculiar hooded man, but her song hit notes of deep morose as she pined for someone or something outside the confines of the scene.

As the first act raced forward, a crescendo rose up from the musicians below. Through the orchestral strains, Ana found her attention drawn toward the intricate set dressing and vivid costumes. Certainly, the Weavers' Guild had had some part in that. Throughout the production, various characters came and went, but the figure in yellow was ever present, haunting each scene with an almost predatory interest. He wore a sort of birdlike masque and was perpetually obscured by the various columns and trellises that comprised the background of the scene.

Right on cue, with a crash of cymbals, a number of dancers sprang onto the stage, each one swathed in brilliant, flowing oranges and reds. They leapt about with balletic precision, driving away the rest of the cast and prancing around the scenery. High up over the stage, they flung fiery batons, leaving a helical trail of flame as they spun through the air. Here and there, they cavorted in their crazed yet graceful display. Suddenly they jumped down off the apron and raced through the crowd, lighting up the patrons' faces with a deep red glow as they ran up the aisles and out into the lobby beyond.

As the music died down, Ana's attention returned to the stage—the cloaked man had departed, and two women were now engaged in conversation in hushed tones. So engaging was the performance that she did not notice the quiet creak of the door behind her seat as a diminutive feline dressed in black slipped through the opening.

Onstage below, the robed figure had returned and was removing his hood. The leading lady recoiled with a blood-curdling scream of terror, and it was at that moment that Ras Dashen leapt up onto the back of Sundry's chair and plunged his knife into her chest.

Her mouth was agape as if gasping in surprise, but the sound of her agony was overshadowed by the scripted chaos onstage.

Inches away, Ana was paralyzed with surprise and confusion. For a moment, she thought she saw Ras Dashen look at her and mouth something like "Sorry" before the lights above the stage were snuffed out and the theater was plunged into darkness.

A cold, sickening dread surged into Ana's gut. Time seemed to slow down, and silence filled her awareness. Far below, the audience surged into applause, but she could hear nothing, save for the rush of her pulse pounding in her ears and the faint rattle of breath as it left Sundry's lifeless frame.

The opening act had concluded. As the houselights came up, Ras Dashen was nowhere to be found.

As Various turned his attention from the stage back to the box to gauge his companions' reactions to the show, his eyes settled on the growing pool of red on Sundry's chest, her body now slumping down in her chair. Likely she would have fallen forward if not for the blade's thorough route through her sternum, exiting her back and pinning her to the seat.

Disbelief flooded his face as he looked first at his love, then at Ana, and back to the seeping red stain on a once immaculate gown.

"Guards," he gasped breathlessly. Then, jumping back from his seat and grasping at the banister, "Guards!"

In moments, two large bipedal canines rushed into the box and paused for a moment to assess the scene.

Ana's shock gave way to anguish. "It was Ras Dashen! I saw him, he was just here, search the hallways, I—"

A large black paw covered her mouth as a burly German shepherd was busy tying her hands behind her back. Her eyes darted back to Various, who had removed the dagger and was now cradling the cold body in his arms, dark teardrops joining the crimson stains on Sundry's dress.

As Ana was being pulled out of the box, the lights grew dim once again, and the curtain began to rise on the second act.

6

A small fan rattled away in the tiny kitchen, drowning out some of the late-summer evening street noise, but not doing much to cool down the room. The green and earthy aroma of fresh basil was punctuated by the sharp and eye-watering sting of Thai chili. Reaching up over the frying pan, Ana stood on her tiptoes to turn on the extractor hood over the stove. Returning to her cutting board on the counter, she began to mince a few cloves of garlic to even out the flavor.

As she stepped back to adjust the temperature, a pair of arms wrapped around her stomach and squeezed her in a tight embrace. Messy blond curls cascaded down Ana's shoulder as Amber placed her chin there gently. She inhaled deeply.

"I love krapow."

"I know," said Ana. "Hand me the fish sauce—it's not funky enough yet."

Amber released her grip and crossed the room to the pantry, digging around the various boxes and condiments. She returned with a small phial and handed it to Ana.

"How was work?" asked Amber.

"Oh, the usual. I think Alison means well, but she doesn't have enough context to be genuinely useful, so she just sets up meetings about random crap, and then we all have to show up and explain to her that whatever she thought the problem was wasn't actually a problem to begin with."

"Mmm. Whatever happened with her and Jerry?"

"I don't really know." Ana knit her brow and gazed up from her work at the stove as she returned the bottle to Amber. "I think the last time we had a staff meeting, they were both there, but I don't think I've had a real conversation with either of them since that company picnic. They were a pretty overt item at the holiday party last year, but I'm thinking maybe that's gone south. I dunno."

Amber returned the sauce to the pantry and crossed back around the table to Ana, placing her hand on Ana's back and lightly scratching back and forth between her shoulder blades.

"James, the guy who works nights, found a bottle of pumpkin spice syrup under a stack of aprons last night," said Amber, chuckling. "That thing's got to be at least half a year old, probably older, since they ship it out starting in, like, August. Anyway, he opened it up and poured it all over one of those breakfast sandwiches that's been sitting in the front case all day, because, quote, 'it's like bougie honey mustard,' then ate the whole thing."

Amber laughed as Ana gagged in disgust.

"Needless to say," Amber continued, "he didn't make his shift this afternoon."

Amber stepped over to a cupboard and retrieved two plates, then walked back over to set the table. Ana spooned out equal portions over rice and then took her seat next to Amber at the table.

Amber brought her hand up across her chest as her gaze met the floor. "So, I'm thinking of getting another tattoo …"

"Oh yeah? What of?"

"I don't really know yet. I don't have a precise idea in my head, I just kind of want one."

"How about my name on your forehead so I'll always be on your mind?" said Ana.

"How about your lips on my butt so you can eat my ass?"

Ana laughed, until she looked up and saw the color draining from Amber's face.

"Hey, are you okay?" she asked urgently.

"Yeah, I'm just feeling kind of nauseous all of a sudden," said Amber, placing her fork down and holding her stomach with a frown.

"Too spicy for you, my delicate princess?" Ana laughed.

"We'll see who's laughing when I make curry tomorrow night," said Amber with a glare.

Outside, the noise and bustle of downtown Seattle continued into the night.

* * *

Ana opened her eyes and found herself staring up at an unfamiliar ceiling. It was still very early, perhaps just before sunrise, and the walls of her cell flickered in pale pinstripes from the oily light of torches on the other side of the bars. She raised her head cautiously from her dingy cot and looked around the room. It was bare save for a chamber pot in the corner and some empty shackles affixed to the wall. A tiny window high in the wall opposite the door seemed to let in some fresh air.

Slowly she rolled onto her side, then drew her legs up and pushed herself into a seated position. Glancing down, she noticed a reddish-brown stain splattered across her previously clean sneakers. At once the sickening image of Sundry pinned to her chair rushed back into her mind. The viscous red fluid surged forth around the dagger's blade as she drew her dying breath. Just beyond her, Various sat motionless, his attention rapt by the spectacle onstage. And there, in the shadows behind the chairs, lurked that insidious cat. His eyes bore into Ana's as he drove the dagger through. "Sorry," he mouthed in silence.

Sliding off the cot onto her feet, she reached into her pockets instinctively. Her phone and wallet were gone, as was the pin she'd received in the alley. Stepping forward to the iron bars, she saw she was in some sort of hallway. The cell across from hers seemed identical in construction, but vacant. The bars were too close together for her to stick her head through, so she could not get a sense of the rest of the hallway.

Last night, a bag had been placed over her head as they had departed the opera house, so she had no idea where she currently was, though from the impeccable craftsmanship of the pale stone walls, she surmised she must still be in Istabar somewhere.

As she started to walk back to the cot, the shadows of the bars on the wall in front of her began to shift in creeping parallax. The room grew steadily brighter, and she could hear footsteps now, padding down the hall. She turned around to await whatever visitor might be coming to her dreary oubliette.

First, a torch came into view. It was held by a large paw covered in white fur. As the guard dog stepped into full view, Ana took stock of the massive Great Pyrenees. He had a large helmet on, a cloak, and a belt, attached to which was a rather impressive-looking scimitar. Hanging off the hilt was a key ring, which, upon arriving at the lock, he removed and began to search.

Flipping through the keys, he spoke at last. "Turn around."

Ana frowned but slowly turned her back to the guard.

"Arms behind your back," he said, reaching through the bars.

Ana knew what was coming. The cold steel manacles closed around her wrists. Withdrawing his paws, he slid one of the keys into the lock, turned it with a click, and pulled the door open on its rusted, creaking hinges. He grabbed Ana's right arm, firmly but surprisingly gently, and led her out of the cell, following the hallway up and around through various labyrinthine twists and turns. Eventually, they came upon a small room, appointed with a table and two chairs. The guard entered the room with Ana and sat her down in one of the chairs.

"Wait here."

He turned and departed the small office. Ana heard a click in the door, followed by footsteps padding slowly away.

Several minutes passed in total silence. Just as Ana considered standing to investigate the chamber further, there was another click in the locking mechanism of the door, and then it swung open to reveal a diminutive but very serious-looking basset hound. This one was wearing some sort of sash, in addition to a scimitar on his belt. The sash was decorated with a number of small medals, which flickered and jingled as he walked in and locked the door behind him.

He pulled out the chair opposite Ana's position and took a seat, placing his paws on the table and gazing into her eyes inquisitively.

"Hello," he said at last. "My name is Charles. I am the captain of the City Guard of Istabar." His eyes were piercing but not unkind. A fringe of white fur dusted his eyes and his muzzle, and his long ears drooped down and rested on the table. "You are Ana, I take it?"

She nodded curtly.

"Well, Ana. Then it is my duty to inform you that you stand accused of the murder of Lady Sundry Quinn, paragon of the Weavers' Guild and sitting member of the Ruling Council of Istabar. If you are found guilty, the punishment for murder is death."

Ana's heart sank as she once again felt a chilling dread seeping into her stomach. With no witnesses, how could she prove her innocence?

"Of course, it's possible we may be able to work out a more lenient sentence if you cooperate with our investigation."

"It wasn't me," Ana blurted out in frustration. "It was Ras Dashen. He came into the box during the end of the first act and stabbed Lady Sundry as the lights went out."

"That is a serious allegation. Ras Dashen has been a trusted merchant in Istabar for many years. You, however, are an outsider who appeared in our city yesterday."

"What possible motive could I have had for killing Lady Sundry? I'm just here to try and find my friend Amber. Ras Dashen gave me the Sirens' Silk as a gift for Lord Various—it was his idea to go to the opera."

Ana paused for a moment as she felt her own voice echo off the barren walls of the room. She took a deep breath, and as she closed her eyes, she could see Sundry's pale corpse cradled in the arms of her anguished husband. Opening her eyes, she continued in a quieter, but no less insistent, tone.

"I'm sorry for what happened. And I'm heartbroken for Lord Various. He has been nothing but kind to me since I arrived in Istabar. But I had nothing to do with Lady Sundry's murder."

Charles examined her face, tilting his head from side to side, then furrowed his brow and stood up from the table. Wordlessly he walked around behind Ana. She heard the jingle of keys and then felt a sudden lightness as the manacles dropped away from her wrists and clattered onto the ground.

"I believe you," he said, still standing just outside Ana's peripheral vision, "but what matters is not what I believe. What matters is the facts. Until we can corroborate your story, you must remain here in the guardhouse."

He walked over to the door to the interrogation chamber and unlocked it with his prodigious key ring. "Follow me; I will show you to the prison yard." He began to walk through the door but then paused and turned back to face Ana. "Oh, and here are your effects. They have been deemed by our examiner to pose no threat to your fellow inmates." He reached into his sash and produced a small bag. Ana took it and opened it to find her phone, wallet, and the tiny pin.

They exited the room and traveled up a flight of stairs. At the top, the hallway opened up into an interior courtyard, with massive, featureless walls on every side. The sun was beginning to rise over the city, coloring the sky a deep navy blue.

"Make yourself at home," said Charles. "You may be here for quite some time."

7

The Ruling Council of Istabar generally convened on the first of each month in a small circular chamber atop the Tower of Drasz. The building—the tallest in Istabar—was located at the very center of the city. The council chamber itself was of simple design. A circular staircase wound up through the floor to a room encircled with broad windows, affording a 360-degree view of the city. Five simple chairs were stationed here, pointed inward. Each chair was emblazoned with the seal of its respective guild: the anvil, the plow, the needle and thread, the shield, and an ornate *D*, the symbol of currency in Istabar.

Today a special session of the council had been called to discuss the tragedy of Lady Sundry's death. As the leader of the Weavers' Guild, and duly elected representative to the council, her empty chair was a stark reminder of the gravity of the situation.

Representing the Bank of Drasz was Lord Benjamin Drasz, a large and grizzled old man with a shaggy, greying beard. He was conversing with Persephone, envoy of the Farmers. Persephone was a diminutive black feline with a lithe disposition despite her advanced years. Across from them, flanked by two empty chairs, sat Carver Olen, a stout and normally boisterous dwarf clad in the livery of the Anvil. Today he remained silent and attentive to his compatriots as they reviewed the facts as they knew them.

"One moment the curtain is open—Lady Sundry is watching the proceedings—and then the lights go out, and she's lying there dead. No one could get in and out so quickly—it has to be that girl," said Benjamin.

"I wouldn't be so quick to pass judgment," said Persephone. "There are those among us who would jump at the chance to sow discontent among the guilds, and some of them are skilled enough to do it." She glanced over at the empty chair next to Olen and sighed. "To think that someone could go to such lengths … to stoop so low …"

"I don't know what this girl's motives are, but she's not from Istabar. She could have been sent here by anyone."

"Or she's simply a convenient patsy," said Persephone. "Either way, we're not going to get to the bottom of this by sitting around in a council chamber, arguing about hearsay."

"She's right." A gruff voice echoed up the stairwell as the council's fourth living member, Captain Charles, ascended into the chamber. "We have a suspect in custody, yes, but we have a great deal more work to do before we can arrange a trial. For starters, according to the eyes of the Weavers, she did not enter the opera house with the murder weapon, so it must have been brought in another way. That means, at the very least, there is an accomplice in play. We don't have many leads, but she asserts that Ras Dashen is involved, so we intend to apprehend and question him when next he returns to Istabar."

"When next he returns?" Persephone crossed her arms. "He just arrived yesterday. Where is he off to so quickly?"

"We don't know, but he and his band departed to the southeast this morning—perhaps back to Harveston for another shipment."

"I think I would know if my own guild was preparing another shipment."

"Regardless, we should not pause proceedings while we wait for Ras Dashen's return," said Benjamin. "I recommend we commence with organizing the hearing. It will take some time for us to gather our chosen deponents. There is also the matter of Lady Sundry's now-vacant council seat."

Olen broke his silence at last. "I reached out to the Weavers' Guild this morning. Evidently, the vote was nearly unanimous in favor of Lord Various's succession to the seat. Unfortunately, Lord Various has been holed up in his office since the incident and is not expected to make an appearance, public or otherwise, for some time."

"Understandable. The poor dear." Persephone sighed. "To have lost your beloved to a senseless assassination and then have the duties of office thrust upon you the very next day … He must be given time to mourn, at the very least."

"Agreed," said Benjamin. "In the meanwhile, the Bank of Drasz is prepared to work with the Weavers to maintain finances and continue production until such time as the seat can be properly filled by Lord Various."

"Very well. Let's put this arrangement to a vote, then," said Olen.

Thus did the temporary leadership of the Weavers' Guild fall to the Bank of Drasz with unanimous agreement.

*   *   *

As the sun set over Istabar, the darkness seemed to pour over the staggeringly high walls and fill up the prison yard like a thimble submerged in ink. Ana sat, back against the wall, picking absentmindedly at the grass as she tried to retrace her steps and map out the hidden labyrinth of cells beneath her.

She had spent the day wandering the prison, searching every nook and cranny for a possible escape route. Loose bars here and there, guard rotations, visitation hours—a puzzle of many disparate pieces, but one she thought she might eventually crack. After all, if Charles was to be believed, she might have all the time in the world.

The chime of a distant bell indicated that the evening guard was about to rotate in. The various hounds stationed in the yard began to make their way over to the guardhouse as their replacements filed out into the field. Ana followed the departing crew down the stairs and into the lower level of the prison, making her way to her cell so as not to be caught out past curfew. As she passed through the various corridors and around the dizzying array of twists and turns, she paused for a moment. A curious breeze was flowing down one of the hallways on her left, which she had not noticed earlier in the day.

She cast a furtive glance around the corridor—there were no inmates in any of the cells in this wing, and the guards had filtered out in the changeover. As she retraced her steps backward, she came upon an irregular opening in the wall. It revealed a corridor that did not appear to be of the same construction as the other hallways—it was much older, less uniform, made of cobblestones, and dappled with mossy specks.

She took a few cautious steps down the disused hallway and was quickly met with the strong, clear scent of pine. Picking up her pace, she followed the clear air around yet more twists and turns until she arrived at what appeared to be a dead end.

The room was bare save for a few small, empty crates and some organic detritus—dead leaves, cobwebs, and the like. It was extremely dark—the sconces in the walls had long since burnt their torches to ash—but a soft shimmer of moonlight splayed across the room, cut up into neat squares.

Ana sighed. She pulled her arms in against the chill of this bleak oubliette and cast her gaze down at the floor, where she noticed a smattering of faintly glowing squares.

Ana's eyes followed the checkerboard pattern across the floor, up the wall, and over to a grating fixed in the ceiling above. There was a padlock on the interior side of the grating that seemed to ward off unintended access to this forgotten wing of the cellblock.

The ceiling here was rather high up—too high to reach directly—so Ana set to work pulling some of the crates around as quietly as she could manage. Placing one box on top of another, she pulled herself up atop the teetering plinth and was able to grasp the iron bars above. Upon closer inspection, and to Ana's great surprise, the padlock was unlocked—it was simply hanging from the grating. Ana pulled the lock off and pushed up on the grating. With some effort, it broke free of its rusty rigor mortis and swung up and away from the frame. Her heart now racing, she gripped the edge of the opening and swung her feet up, catching one on the exterior surface and slowly pulling herself through the aperture.

Out here, the fresh night air was crisp and cool, and the wind moved through the grass like a gentle whisper. Ana looked up to find herself on the opposite side of Istabar's massive wall. The small grating was built into a hillside some twenty or thirty feet away from the foot of the wall and was concealed at the base of a tree by a stand of low shrubs.

There's no way no one's found that grating before. How did it get unlocked?

But Ana had no time to meditate on the miraculous circumstances of her escape. She knew it was only a matter of time before the guards noticed her absence.

Carefully she eased the grating back to its original position and slid the padlock through the space between the iron bars and the frame. She slid the shank of the lock back through the hasp eyelet and closed it with an audible click, sealing the exit.

Shielded only by the cover of darkness, she then stood and began her sprint for the tree line. Vaulting over small roots and clumps of foliage, she raced toward the phalanx of trees. The wind rushing past her ears muted the sound of the city behind her, but she dared not slow down to check for evidence of pursuit.

As she reached the edge of the pine forest, her manic pace finally began to slow. Ducking behind a large tree some four or five yards into the timber, she stood, panting, and turned back to take stock of her location.

In front of her, in the center of the valley, stood the imposing wall, buildings peeking out above its impenetrable face and climbing the jagged stone cliffs into the blackened sky above. She saw now that she was on the opposite side of the valley from where she had entered—the river winding down its center was now to her left, waterfall on the right, indicating that she was headed farther east. *Amber came through the Westward Gate*, she recalled. *Perhaps she continued east as well ...*

Here, in the dense pine thicket, there was no clear pathway, and the canopy above let little light in through the tightly packed clumps of needles. As the adrenaline of her flight from Istabar slowly faded and the heat in her veins died away, she became suddenly aware of the chill wind moving through the trees, urging her along. Taking one last look at the glittering city to which she could no longer return, she gathered her courage and set off into the woods.

8

na had been trudging through the forest for what seemed like several hours. The fear of being apprehended had slowly abated as she put more and more difficult terrain between herself and Istabar. In its place, however, was an ever-deepening sense of isolation. The pine forest was dark, almost unnaturally so. She hoped she was moving at least in a straight line, but the constant circumnavigation of the densely packed trees made a sure trajectory very difficult to maintain.

There was a deep silence here that rendered her footsteps over the dead forest floor as near-deafening crunches. Periodically she would pause to get her bearings, and in those moments, the sounds of the woods would increase in resolution to the extent that she could just make out the myriad chitters, warbles, and hoots of distant nocturnal beasts. Every so often, she would disturb some creature in the dry pine needles below, and a frantic scuttle of debris would shoot out and away from her path, but so far, nothing had been so curious as to make its presence known.

As she continued through the forest, the gradient of the land changed ever so slightly. She could now tell that she was headed downhill. She decided to follow this downward pitch in the hope of finding some woodland pathway or perhaps a small stream that might lead to civilization. *Will Istabar have sent someone ahead?* she wondered. *How badly do they want to find me?*

As she continued, the grade of the descent increased, and she found herself grasping at the sticky pine branches to maintain her footing. Suddenly she slipped and began to slide down the hill, tumbling end over end and rolling over stumps and small rocks as she struggled to slow her fall. She flew over a low cliff at the bottom of the hill and landed in a shallow gully with a loud "Oof!"

Strangely, the drop had not felt as sudden as she had expected. Indeed, reaching down to push herself up off the ground, she realized she was not on the ground at all but in fact suspended several feet above it in a curious stringy net. As she rolled about and struggled to right herself, she became more and more tangled in the sticky substance, until at last the creeping realization dawned on her.

Freezing instantly, she cast her attention into the dark reaches of the forest. Where once there was a subtle undercurrent of small creatures rummaging around in the night, now there was only silence. Carefully, quietly, she attempted to free her arms from the sticky webbing, but her struggle had rendered movement almost impossible. Hanging helplessly, she breathed in deeply in an attempt to calm her racing heart. The wind had died down, but there was a slight hint of ash in the air, as though perhaps a distant campfire was burning out its final embers. Though she remained motionless, Ana was wrestling within, weighing the risk of being apprehended against the threat of her current predicament. At last she decided to break her silence.

"Help … help!" she cried into the dark. The forest swallowed her voice. "HELP! SOMEONE HELP ME!" she shouted again, staring into the void for any hint of movement or activity.

After a few moments, a response came—not from below but from above. A curious sickly hissing sound penetrated through the darkness and sent her heart racing once again. Down toward the web from high above slithered an enormous black shape, blotting out what meager moonlight filtered through the canopy. As it grew closer and closer to Ana's face, she could begin to make out its details. The countenance lowering toward her was covered with black, beady eyes. Beneath the eyes were two mandibles, slick with some dark, viscous ichor. Behind this twisted visage were four pendulous legs hanging down, covered in bristling hair and beginning to grasp toward their prey. The other four legs were bent back above its bulbous abdomen, steadying the descent. A dark spinneret pumped out sticky fluid, which hardened in the air into a ropelike silk.

Now mere feet from her exposed throat, the gargantuan arachnid opened its jaws, foaming with hunger. Black, caustic saliva dripped down onto Ana's face, oozing into her mouth and replacing her screams of terror with frantic coughing and retching. The spider's forelegs began to close around her wriggling body as the creature reared up for the killing blow.

Suddenly it recoiled in shock as an arrow sailed up from below, plunging into its ponderous underbelly and spilling out putrid offal. It bucked and hissed, clambering back up the tether and disappearing into the trees above as two more arrows sailed up into the darkness.

For the first time in what seemed like an eternity, Ana sensed a glowing warmth, a light in the darkness that rose up to meet her from the ground below. A large hand grasped her and pulled her down, the sinuous webbing slowly snapping and breaking away. A cloaked figure stood over her, backlit by the light, and small creatures worked all around her to cut away the remaining silk and free her arms and legs at last.

Ana rolled onto her side and vomited into the mess of pine needles and cast-off webbing. She tried to speak, but the effort was too great for her shivering body. The warm glow swung down to meet her face, and in its light, she could see the stony visage of a great wooden skull above her, pocked with errant barnacles and the occasional strand of seaweed. A large, bony hand dipped down under the small of her back and hefted her onto a gentle shoulder as the world faded once more into darkness.

9

The quiet rhythm of the road rumbling beneath the tires of Ana's boxy mid-1990s station wagon played perfect accompaniment to the staccato patter of rain on the windshield. The wiper blades swung forth, wiping away a fragment of the sky, then jittered back across the scene, painting glimmering hexagons behind the brake lights ahead. Progress was slow going, but Ana didn't mind—she could spend hours alone in the car on a quiet night like this, away from the troubles of the world and safely ensconced in a soft bubble of rain and city lights.

As she gazed into the inky night before her, her phone began to buzz in her pocket. Shifting to the side, she dug it out and put the call on speaker, placing the phone into her cupholder and focusing once again on the road.

"Hey, how'd it go today?"

"It was fine." Amber's voice was warm and soothing, even over the tinny attenuation of a subpar cell signal. "James came to work half in the bag again. Big surprise. We should just assume that nobody's going to show up the morning after New Year's and close the café, but you know."

"I mean about the doctor's office," said Ana. "How was it?"

"Oh, nothing special. They looked at me, I peed in a cup, they told me I'm normal."

"You're the least normal person I have ever met. You better go back and get a second opinion."

Amber snorted. "Are you coming home soon or what? I might die from hunger. Then my death would be on your hands."

"The flight got in a little late. I'm, like … twenty minutes away still."

"Uhhgg," Amber moaned dramatically. "Okay, well, I'm ordering a pizza, and if it's cold by the time you get here, then that's just a reflection of your poor life choices and/or comeuppance for making me wait until ten p.m. to eat dinner."

"Fine, but it better be barbecue chicken and ranch."

"You're disgusting, but fine."

"I love you," said Ana in saccharine singsong.

"Barf."

The car continued down the highway, downtown Seattle looming in the distance, fractured and filtered through tiny prisms on the windshield. Ana reached for the radio and pressed the volume knob. The display sprang to life and flooded the car with a warm glow. A spirited debate between two NPR panelists rolled back and forth across the speakers as the rain began to pour.

*　　*　　*

The scent of smoke and fresh cedar slowly blossomed into Ana's awareness. The distant whoop of some avian sentinel echoed through the trees. As she opened her eyes, she felt a moment of panic as her arms lay pinned to her sides. Looking down, she found it was not webbing or rope, but a simple blanket wrapped around her body. She wriggled free one of her arms, reached out, and slowly pushed herself off the ground, leaning back against a fallen log and staring dazedly into the flames of the campfire in front of her.

It seemed perhaps midmorning, though the sky was muted grey with billowing clouds. A gentle drizzle pattered on a leather tarp above her, funneling the rainwater into a nearby barrel. The sound of frogs echoed through the leaves, suggesting a nearby pond or lake.

As Ana continued to take stock of her environment, she heard a deep and resonant voice behind her. "Ah, you're awake."

She turned, still seated, to see Doro exiting a large tent behind her, carrying what appeared to be a tiny basket.

"You will have to excuse me—the birds of this area do not lay the largest of eggs … but I think we will be able to make something of this nonetheless."

He bent down and sat next to her, sitting cross-legged, as appeared to be his norm. From the basket, he produced a handful of small elliptical eggs in dappled greys and blues. "I will have to ask for your help here, I'm afraid. My hands lack the dexterity for such a task." He held up an enormous skeletal hand as evidence. Reaching over to the firepit, Doro picked up the iron skillet resting above the flames and held it in front of Ana.

Ana, for her part, gently took an egg and then leaned forward over the skillet. With some effort, she cracked the egg on the rim and emptied the contents into the pan. The egg immediately began to sizzle and cook atop the hot iron. After throwing the shell into the fire beyond, she continued through the rest of the eggs as Doro took up a spoon and scrambled the whites and the yolks together. He placed the pan back onto the griddle over the fire and continued his stirring, adding in some pepper from his basket and periodically inspecting the progress with his spoon.

After a few more moments, he removed the pan from the flames and placed it on the ground between himself and Ana. He set out the salt and pepper from his basket and handed Ana the spoon. She ate gingerly at first, and then with renewed vigor, as Doro watched the flames dance in silence.

"I owe you an apology," he said. "I should never have let you go into the theater alone. When I heard what had happened, I went straight over, but they would not let me into the prison to see you."

"It wasn't your fault." Ana placed the spoon back down in the skillet. "And anyway, I'd be dead if it wasn't for you." She shivered, the shape of those dread mandibles still fresh in her mind. "How did you find me out here?"

"You are very loud."

"But what are you doing here? And where are we?"

Doro sat and gazed into the dying embers of the breakfast fire. "I heard whispers that feline merchant was involved, so I went to look for him. Finding such a creature is not easy in the wilderness, so I came here for help." Doro gestured around at the various rocks and piles of leaves that littered the campsite. "I have many friends here, and I came to ask them if they had seen him on the East Road. We were discussing the matter when I heard you falling down the hill over there."

Ana looked around at the clearing. As far as she could tell, it was empty save for Doro and herself.

"But there's no one else here," said Ana.

"Perhaps no one else you recognize, but the forest is very much alive," said Doro. "Cromag, Gorthek, I would like to introduce you to my friend Ana."

At the mention of these appellations, a low pile of rocks and a mess of fallen branches and leaves began to stir. They gathered themselves up as if by magic into the forms of stout bipedal creatures and walked stiffly over to Ana's seat by the fire. They bowed deeply and then walked behind Doro and entered the tent. A few moments later, they returned, both sporting a simple quiver of arrows and a bow of wood and vine.

"Elementals, you see," said Doro, inspecting their quivers with a nod of approval. "They guard the natural places of this world and can be found in any such place where the wilds have need of protection."

Ana marveled at the diminutive constructs making their way around camp, tidying the area and fastidiously cleaning up debris. "They are excellent marksmen, these two—but alas, not the sharpest of lookouts. They do not believe they have seen Ras Dashen along this road, though they admit to paying little heed to that which does not threaten the woods."

Ana grimaced at the mention of Ras Dashen's name. "That rat bastard can rot in hell. He set me up to take the fall for Lady Sundry's death, and unless I manage to find him somehow, I'll probably never be able to set foot in Istabar again. As long as Lord Various thinks I killed his wife, he'll never help me find Amber."

"There may yet be a way to save Lady Sundry," said Doro.

"Save? From what? She died when Ras Dashen ran his dagger through her heart." Even now, the thought of it made her sick.

"When a soul is ripped from its body, its journey to eternity is not immediate." Doro lowered his voice and beckoned Ana closer. She stood slowly, uneasily at first but then confident in her balance. "There is a place," Doro continued, "where lost souls go to make their peace with death. A great monument lies not too far north of here. We may yet be able to right this grievous wrong. But we will need tools."

"What kind of tools?" Ana whispered, mystified.

"The Relics of Life and Death."

10

The bright and colorful banners that normally hung proudly from the rooftops and balustrades of Istabar had been replaced with black tapestries of mourning. In the streets, the normally bustling and boisterous atmosphere had been supplanted by a somber and mournful tone. The bazaar, traditionally the center of activity in the city, was practically deserted—the people of Istabar had instead begun to congregate in the northern quarter of the city. There, in the center of an expansive open plaza, was an enormous basin. It was fashioned as a sort of vesica piscis, into which drained various aqueducts, forming a shimmering colonnade of water. The eye-shaped pool was bordered on one side by a small step, allowing easy access to the calf-deep crystal waters, and on the other side, a series of ornate archways hewn into the city's prodigious wall led to a precipitous drop into the waterfall below.

Floating in the pool, moored to a gilded pole in the center of the plaza, was a small canoe crafted of pale birchwood. It bobbed up and down gently in the ever-shifting water. The gathered throng had come to see the boat—to see if what they'd heard could possibly be true. One by one, starting at the back of the crowd, the onlookers began to part and make way for a path clear down the center to the small boat.

At first the procession was led by a black-cloaked priest bearing the insignia of the Weavers' Guild. The gentle burbling of the falling water was soon accompanied by the shimmer of chimes and the drone of deep metal bells. One by one, the funeral party entered the plaza and took up its place at the side of the pool, until at last a figure appeared at the end of the procession.

Lord Various Quinn was dressed in a dazzling coat of pure night, bereft of moon or stars. His platinum hair cascaded down his shoulders like a moonlit river at midnight. His ice-blue eyes flashed with barely managed anguish under a veneer of stiff restraint. In his arms, he held the corpse of Lady Sundry Quinn, swaddled in a gown made of pure Sirens' Silk.

A collective gasp rushed through the crowd.

Slowly he stepped up to the edge of the water, then down into the pool, holding Sundry just above the rippling surface, her gown dipping into the turbulent currents below. His coat spread out on the water behind him like a viscous, shimmering oil.

He walked up to the side of the moored canoe, then gently laid her lifeless body down on the boat, placing his hand upon her collarbone, eyes closed, in a final goodbye. It was only a moment, but to the onlookers on the shore, it could have been an eternity.

Various turned away from the boat and stepped back up onto the cool, slick stone floor of the plaza. The bells and chimes ceased, leaving only the quiet shifting of the water echoing through the air.

Drawing a deep breath, he spoke. "No one yet lives who does not know the name Sundry Quinn. When I met her, I was just a boy, and she was Sundry Drasz, daughter of an empire and heiress to a grander legacy than I could ever have imagined. And yet she gave all of that up to serve in the humble craft of leadership. No one has set foot in Istabar who has not benefited from her gentle guidance, and for that, we all owe her a debt that can never be repaid.

"Two nights ago, Lady Sundry's life was taken by a coward, a villain who deserves less than a footnote in today's proceedings. But be it known that such acts of barbarous hatred will be repaid a thousandfold. Tomorrow we will consign her murderer to a fate worse than death, as payment for that which cannot be indemnified. But today we celebrate a life immaculately lived, and mourn the passing of a soul too bright for song and too brave for story."

At this, Various drew from his side a gleaming saber and held it up in the air for all to see the light glinting off its impossibly sharp edge. "And so we consign this lifeless vessel to the sea, that her soul may be granted solace from the trappings of mortality, and respite from the tragedy of her passing."

He brought the sword down and sliced clean through the rope holding the boat to the mooring post. It began to drift toward the precipice and was soon carried swiftly over the edge, tumbling into the turbulent waters and jagged rocks below.

After sheathing his sword, Various walked briskly out of the plaza to the sound of bells and chimes as the people of Istabar returned in somber contemplation to their homes.

*   *   *

Looking out over the city from his office atop the Weavers' Guild, Various sighed. The elevator door slid open silently behind him, and out stepped Cornelius and Captain Charles. The pair passed through the small receiving room and into the office proper. Offering a hand toward the desk, Cornelius stepped back and took a seat in the waiting room outside. After a few moments, Charles cleared his throat.

"You wished to speak with me in private, Lord Various?"

Various did not turn around; his gaze remained fixed out of the window, pointed toward the impenetrable walls of the prison. "Yes, Captain. The time has come for that iniquitous wretch in your charge to pay for her crimes. I would ask that you bring her to me."

"My heart is broken for you, Lord Various. I, along with every creature with a soul in Istabar, was truly moved by your speech today. You know I would do anything in my power to right this wrong. But releasing prisoners to their accusers is not in my power. The laws of this city—"

"Charles." Various turned at last to face the captain. His eyes flashed with fierce determination. "I am not interested in excuses; I am interested in justice. And until such time as that justice is served, this city stands upon a knife-edge. The slightest misstep on behalf of any of us could jeopardize the future of Istabar forever. Help me deliver justice, or the people will learn that all it takes to seize power is a knife in the dark and an opportune moment."

"Justice, Various?" Charles raised an eyebrow. "Or vengeance?"

Stepping forward, Various took a seat at his desk. He hung his head and rested his brow upon his right hand. His left sat balled in a tight fist.

"And in any case," Charles continued, "the Guard will deliver justice—through a fair trial." Charles's face softened, and he reached up to place a paw on Various's shoulder. "Lady Sundry's murderer will be held accountable for the tragedy they have wrought. I will see to it personally. But it must happen according to the laws of our society, or we shall stand no surer in our virtue than those who wish to divide us."

Various stared down at the table, his knuckles white with frustration. Slowly his hand relaxed, and his shoulders dropped.

He sighed as he rose up and slumped back into his chair. "Very well. Thank you for your diligence in this matter, Charles. It is much appreciated."

Charles nodded and turned to make his way back to the elevator.

"By the way, Charles, did you perchance find anything out of the ordinary among her effects?"

The captain stopped and stood silently for a moment. He turned back around to look upon the figure seated at the desk.

"Nothing out of the ordinary," he replied.

Various studied the basset hound's face, following the wrinkles and whiskers with thoughtful precision. "Very well. Would you be so kind as to inform the council that I appreciate Drasz's attention to the affairs of the Weavers' Guild until such time as I feel fit to take up my duties as councillor?"

"Of course, Lord Various." Charles bowed deeply and took his leave. As the elevator doors closed behind him, Cornelius stepped forward into the office.

"He's up to something, my lord. Our agents inside the prison have not made contact with Ana all day."

Various drummed his fingers upon the glass surface of his immaculate desk. "Bring me Ras Dashen."

11

Ana, Doro, Gorthek, and Cromag had been walking through the forest for the better part of a day. Gradually the rain had let up, but the sky was no less dreary, and the air was thick with humidity. The small woodland trail they were following eventually joined a larger dirt road, which opened up into a clearing on the bank of a stream. There was a simple cobblestone bridge here, and as they crossed it, Doro turned to Ana and spoke.

"This stream is but one of many that form the Wandering River delta. As we cross this bridge, we leave the domain of Istabar and enter the Gyrewood, a shifting swampland of long shadows and forgotten monuments. Stay close—the way is easily lost here. And be on your guard—there are worse things than hungry spiders in these trees."

Ana nodded and closed the distance between herself and Doro. Even as he spoke, the air seemed to close in around them and swallow up their voices.

"Where are we headed, exactly?" asked Ana.

"To the center of the Gyrewood. Most of these lowlands are a twisting maze of bogs and thickets, but at the center, there is a hill called Malthor's Mound. Legends say it is the burial site of a wicked man who lived long ago."

"What made him so wicked?"

"He flirted with some of the darkest powers of this land in search of personal gain. He promised many the gift of eternal life, but in return, he beset them with a myriad of terrible curses. Some were smart enough to turn down his offer; others, lucky enough to meet their end in some other violent fashion. But a few remain to this day, driven mad by the millennia of ceaseless torment brought upon them through their greed and lack of foresight."

Ana shuddered. "So how is he going to help us rescue Lady Sundry?"

"On the top of Malthor's Mound, there is a great swamp oak. It was planted there many ages ago as a ward against Malthor's insidious magic, and there it still stands. As spirits make their way out of this world, they often pass by the swamp oak. If Lady Sundry's spirit is still out there somewhere, we may be able to call her back to this world. But we will need some tools."

"The Relics of Life and Death?"

"Indeed. The Relic of Death is straightforward. We will write down an account of Lady Sundry's death. Most spirits do not know they are dead, so this will help to jog her memory. The Relic of Life is a bit trickier. We will need to find or fabricate something that will remind her of her old life. A drawing of a loved one, perhaps, or a map of Istabar …"

Ana frowned—her drawing skills were questionable at best.

"Normally, a treasured item would be best, but our options here are limited."

At this, Ana's eyes lit up. "I think I might have something."

Reaching into her pockets, she fished around for a moment and then produced the tiny needle-and-thread pin. She offered the item to Doro, who took it in his oversize hands and paused along the trail as he inspected it. Suddenly he brought his head back in surprise and seemed transfixed by the small, simple clasp.

"Where did you find this?" he asked, cradling it reverently in his wooden palms.

"She gave it to me when we met in the streets of Istabar, though I didn't know it was her at the time."

Doro shifted his gaze to Ana and tilted his head, mystified. "This is the Signet of the Weavers' Guild. It identifies the bearer as the rightfully chosen council member on behalf of the guild. Without it, no new councillor can be appointed."

Ana's eyes grew wide. "Why would she give that to me?"

"I do not know," said Doro. "But it is a very precious treasure indeed, and certainly, it would be a fine choice for our purposes today." With great veneration, he handed the pin back to Ana. "Keep it safe. We will need it in the trial to come."

Turning back to the trail, the two continued onward through the ever-deepening marshlands. As they rounded another corner, they came upon a large tree trunk that had been carved in the manner of a grotesque creature, sticking out its tongue and rolling its eyes.

"These totems were carved by the locals that once lived here," said Doro. "They were intended as a warning to keep the unwary from wandering too far into the Gyrewood."

As they continued past the wooden effigy, Ana looked up at her traveling companion. "Doro, you didn't hear anything about Amber while you were out looking for Ras Dashen, did you?"

"Alas, I have not found any further clues as to her present location, though I do have an idea of how we might discover more. While you were at the opera that night in Istabar, I took it upon myself to seek out Carver Olen, the representative to the council on behalf of the Anvil. The Anvil are crafters responsible for creating buildings, infrastructure, tools, and artifacts of all kinds."

As they continued deeper into the mire, Cromag and Gorthek each removed an arrow from their quivers and nocked them to their bows, moving silently through the undergrowth.

"There is a particular artifact of great utility for finding missing persons," Doro continued. "It's called a Periapt of Pursuit, and few now remain who can recall the secrets of its construction, but Olen is one such artisan. In order to—"

Doro's explication was cut short by the sudden alert of the elementals ahead. Cromag and Gorthek stood stock-still, bows drawn back and ready to loose, training their sights on a figure just around a stand of trees.

Doro slowly approached, Ana following just behind.

As they rounded the corner, a wire-thin creature of bone and loose skin shambled toward them. Matted knee-length grey hair sprouted sporadically from its head, its eye sockets sunken and cheekbones sharp. It was draped in some sort of robe, though the garment had long since been reduced to tattered ribbons. Its skin was an awful grey and its extremities shook as it came closer to the party, step by stilted step.

"One of the Accursed," Doro whispered, a pang of sympathy in his voice.

He stepped forward, past the elementals, and raised his staff high, illuminating the pathway with his lantern and catching the creature's pitch-black eyes in its light. Its head jerked forward as it hissed, spraying a cloud of spittle into the air.

"Child of the Gyrewood, I humbly offer to light your path, so that you may return from whence you came," called Doro.

"Fah! You see but shreds and tatters. You know nothing of the light," it sneered. "I have walked these paths for a thousand years. I will walk them for a thousand more. Your sea wood will rot away, Shepherd of Hope. And you," he hissed at Ana, "your blood will sate my dinner guests, and your bones will tend my garden."

"Why such anger, young one?" asked Doro.

At this, the creature rose up and bellowed at the travelers. Ana shrank back behind her companions, but Doro remained unmoved. Its shrieking voice began to shrivel and crack as its body quaked at the exertion. Suddenly it flopped onto the ground and began crawling toward them, scrabbling up onto Doro's robes and weeping in supplication.

"Please, please, I beg of you. Please. Take this gift away from me. I cannot see another sunrise amongst the living."

Doro brushed him aside with his staff and motioned for the rest to follow. "This curse is not for me to lift. None among the living can claim such judgment."

As Doro moved past, Ana followed close behind. She gazed down at the creature and, for the first time, saw its face was streaked with black tears. "I'm sorry," she mumbled as she hurried along.

Up ahead, Cromag and Gorthek watched warily with arrows still trained on the wretched creature as it lay crumpled up beside the trail, wailing into the mud.

*   *   *

As twilight fell on the Gyrewood, a chorus of tree frogs sprang to life amid the dense cattail thickets on the edge of the path. In the distance, the call of a solitary loon echoed through the trees.

"It's getting dark," said Ana. "I take it we're not getting out of here anytime soon."

"That's what the tent is for," said Doro.

As the four travelers continued to weave back and forth across the labyrinth of pathways, they began to hear a deep rumbling sound—at first like a faraway train, and then, as they drew closer, like a regular groan of wind through the trees. At last they walked out into a small clearing in the swamp to find an enormous creature, caked in mud from head to toe. It appeared at first to be an enormous living mound, softly rising and falling with sonorous snoring, but then Ana noticed a face, and arms and legs, bloated and misshapen, but human nonetheless.

As the light from Doro's lantern expanded into the clearing, the large figure coughed and awoke with a start, its mounds of flesh jiggling back and forth with a sickening slosh.

"Who comes to visit the mighty Brodas?" it moaned, flapping its limbs in the mud but unable to stand or otherwise move out from under the weight of its prodigious stomach.

"Only the Shepherd, and my traveling companions," said Doro.

"And to what do I owe the privilege of such an esteemed guest?" asked Brodas with mock deference.

"We are merely passing through to the mound."

"You do me wrong, Shepherd," Brodas cried. "All who wish to see the mound must proffer a token of their gratitude for surviving my court." As Brodas spoke, a wary tree frog began to inch its way across the mud. Instantly a lard-laden hand shot out and grabbed the frog, then brought it up to the mouth. In it went, consumed whole. "Food, perhaps? Have you any bread? Or cheese? Or olives, perhaps?"

"It is your greed that traps you here, Brodas. To help you dig yourself further into such a debt would betray my conscience."

Brodas's arms flailed about wildly as Doro and Ana moved in a wide circle around the heaving pile of flesh. On the opposite side of the clearing, they continued on through the ever-darkening woods. Behind them, they could hear the wails and cries of Brodas as it spat curses after its erstwhile visitors.

"You make a powerful enemy this day, Shepherd!" it screamed. "Your carelessness will be your downfall!"

12

The night was deep and filled with hidden life. Wild chirps and hoots accompanied the crunch of footsteps on fallen leaves. Progress was more arduous now, as the darkness closed in on all sides; the only source of light was Doro's lantern, flickering softly in defiance of the night. They had wandered through innumerable twists and turns in the woods until at last they rounded a final corner and walked out into a broad clearing. Something had prevented the trees here from growing up the hill, as if the foliage itself kept a wide berth.

Ana gazed up at the small mound before them. At its summit, there was a lone oak tree, haggard and barren, but a scant few leaves hinted at life still stirring within.

"We're here," said Doro. "Malthor's Mound."

As Ana started up the hill, there was a sudden rustling behind them. Looking back, Ana saw a pair of eyes gleaming in the lantern light—it seemed the emaciated wretch had followed them through the maze of trees.

"Pay them no mind," said Doro. "We are here for one reason only."

As they crossed the clearing toward the mound, Ana noticed a curious light that danced across the murky bog surrounding them.

"In a place like this, it is not uncommon to witness wandering souls," said Doro. "Spirits that have not yet found the will to continue their journey to eternity. These will-o'-the-wisps congregate around the mound, as do moths around a lantern."

Slowly more and more lights flickered into view, shifting and floating just above the water, each in the image of a soft, pale flame dancing in slow motion. In the distance, Ana could now see tremendous clouds of these souls, floating aimlessly around above the hill, circling in a great waltz as they haunted the night sky.

Step by step, Doro and Ana made their way up the mound while Cromag and Gorthek stood watch below. The dirt was hard packed, and vegetation was sparse—a curious blight amid the otherwise verdant landscape. At the top, Ana was at last afforded her first full view of the Gyrewood, lit by the dancing spirits above. It stretched out as far as the eye could see in every direction, twisting and turning in an impossible maze of trees and water.

Looking back at it now, she mused, it was incredible they'd found their way through at all, much less in the span of only an evening.

"Over here," said Doro, standing beside the ancient oak tree. "It is time we made our case."

Producing a roll of parchment, a quill, and an inkpot from his robes, he handed the accoutrements to Ana. "Remember, we must tell the story of Lady Sundry's untimely demise. Keep it brief but descriptive. We must jog her memory as best we can."

Ana held the paper in her hand, the wind gently pulling at its edges. She looked up at the tree, then knelt down in the sparse grass and began to write. She wrote of the beautiful opera house, the opulent interior, the curious play in a language she could not understand. She wrote of the cat in black robes, the swell of the orchestra, the knife in the dark. She wrote of the deep crimson stain on the opera gown and the anguish writ large across Lord Various's face. She wrote of a young woman dragged off against her will to a dank prison cell, left there to rot.

She stood once again and dusted off her knees. Stepping over small rocks and roots, she made her way over to the oak tree. As she held the parchment up to the bark, she reached into her pocket and produced the small needle-and-thread pin. In one swift movement, she drove the pin through the paper and into the bark of the tree. Slowly she stepped back and stood next to Doro. For several minutes, they waited in silence.

Eventually, Ana spoke. "What happens now?"

"Lady Sundry's spirit may find her way to this mound. If she does, she may find these relics and return to us. It is not a sure thing, but as long as they remain here, there is a chance."

"How long will that take?"

Doro's skull was motionless, but Ana detected a frown nonetheless. "I'm afraid I do not know. In the meantime, perhaps you would like to assist me in setting up this tent."

As the two unrolled the fabric and erected some tent poles, the swirl of souls continued to churn above, casting a shimmering glow across the mound and illuminating a simple plaque set into the top of the hill a few feet away from the tree. Ana walked over and crouched down to examine it.

Here lies Malthor, Lord of Lies.
May his promises live no longer than his memory.

Ana stood and turned back to Doro.

The breath was stolen from her lungs. Behind him stood that horrid creature, riddled with arrows, oozing a dark ichor into the dirt. And behind the emaciated wretch crawled a dozen more, each more misshapen than the last, writhing forward with a speed that defied their decrepitude.

"Behind you!" she shouted.

Doro spun around, but it was too late. They leaped upon him like a pack of rabid dogs, scratching at his face and scrabbling up his wooden limbs. He bucked and swung about, but as quickly as he flung them off, more began to jump up and pull him down toward the ground.

"Help!" Ana screamed into the dark. "Cromag! Gorthek! Help!" Down at the bottom of the hill, the elementals were overrun with ancient vestiges of a long-forgotten bargain. Fighting valiantly against the swarm, their battle was nearing its inevitable conclusion. Grasping hands pulled Cromag apart rock by rock as rotting teeth gnashed through Gorthek's vines until the pair were reduced to little more than rubble, dust, and scattered leaves.

Running up to Doro, Ana grabbed onto one of the writhing creatures and attempted to pull it off his back. Craning its neck around, it gnashed its teeth and chomped viciously at her face.

"Ana!" Doro shouted, struggling against the grasping claws of the Accursed. "Get behind the tree and cover your ears!" Letting go of the creature, she ran back behind the oak tree as Doro raised his staff high above his head. "I am Doromondas, Shepherd of Hope! Begone from this place of despair—your lives are not mine to take."

Driving his staff into the ground, a brilliant white light flashed out, blinding in its intensity. A thunderous explosion of air rushed out from the point of impact, throwing twisted creatures off the mound in all directions and driving a deep crack into the earth. The ground under Ana's feet began to shift and crumble, and she grabbed out for one of the limbs on the old oak tree, but to no avail.

The earth gave way beneath her, and she tumbled and slid down into the stone of the mound. Rubble and debris rained down behind her, filling in the hole as she fell feet-first into a dark chamber under the hill. She hit the ground hard and rolled to a stop on a dank stone floor. Sand and rocks continued to clatter down the precipitous breach and into the room as the opening filled in completely.

Ana lay there for a moment in silence. The room was pitch-black; she could see nothing. Digging into her pocket, she found her phone, screen cracked and broken. But a press of the power button brought the screen flickering to life, revealing a few minutes of energy left in the dying battery. She turned the device around upon her environment to illuminate the room in a soft white glow.

It was a small chamber, dome-like in shape, with what looked like hundreds of thousands of little runes carved into the walls. In the center of the room was a waist-high stone plinth, atop which she could see some sort of figure lying, arms crossed, in funerary repose. Her eyes moved up from the body and toward the ceiling, where the roots of the great oak tree above had penetrated the chamber. Above her, in the ceiling, was a graven hole, an access way up to the top of the mound, now filled in completely in the wake of Doro's cataclysmic blast.

"Doro!" she cried into the darkness above. "Can you hear me? I'm below you!"

Her voice was met with only silence.

Turning her attention back to the figure on the dais, she approached cautiously. The roots stretched down through the ceiling, into the room, and right down to the remains of this ancient corpse. Edging closer, she could see now that the roots plunged directly into the chest of this decrepit husk and deep into the stone slab below him. Other tendrils spread out and wrapped around the neck, the arms, and the legs. His arms were crossed below the breach in his sternum, and in his hands he grasped a sword in a gilded sheath encrusted with gems.

"Malthor," she whispered, "I think I need this now more than you do." Carefully she reached out and began to pry his bony fingers away from the hilt, one by one. A few snapped off and fell into the rib cage, so far gone was the skeleton's sinew. At last the sword was free. She lifted it up and away from the body carefully and laid it across her forearm as she inspected its construction.

It was grand and ornate on the exterior of the scabbard, but the hilt was simple and clean. The pommel was socketed with an enormous crystal of some sort—possibly quartz—and as she held the grip, it glowed slightly. Soon its radiance eclipsed that of her dying cell phone and brought a cool luminosity to the room. The cross guard was simple in construction, with clean geometric lines fashioned of what appeared to be golden metal, and the blade had an open channel running up the length until just shy of the tip.

Removing it from the sheath altogether, Ana swung it about through the air. It whistled and sang as it sliced back and forth—incredibly light for how substantial the blade appeared.

Sliding it back carefully into the scabbard, she held on to the grip as the light flickered along the walls. Searching back and forth, she scanned the runes flowing along the curved walls of the chamber. At first they all seemed random and unintelligible, but a set of rough-hewn characters caught her eye. At once she realized these were strangely angled block letters, and they spelled out words in English:

"SWORD … CROWN … KINGDOM," read one corner of the vast tapestry of words. Elsewhere on the walls were carved "BRIDGE … WALL … CASTLE." Still elsewhere on the ceiling: "FOOD … LOVE … HOPE."

Ana's eyes descended to the stone dais upon which rested the brittle remains of Malthor. In the much-improved illumination cast by the sword, she could now make out a small inscription set into the side of the plinth.

I am forged by the skilled, so too the inept.
I need only my name to be spoken.
I can only be given as long as I'm kept.
I can only be lost if I'm broken.

A riddle—the answer to which, it seemed, had evaded Malthor. At some point, he appeared to have resigned himself to his fate and expired upon the slab, never discovering the answer. *Perhaps*, Ana thought, *this is a test. Perhaps if I succeed where he failed, one of us might still leave this chamber alive …*

Ana knelt down and sat on the floor, gazing up at the constellation of letters across the ceiling. The sword glowed gently in her lap. *Anyone can make it. It can only be given away if it's kept …* Ana recalled the plaque high above, on the top of the hill. *Here lies Malthor, Lord of Lies …* And suddenly it came to her. It seemed so obvious in retrospect, she wondered how it could have possibly eluded Malthor in his final hours.

"A promise," she whispered.

At first nothing happened. But slowly, from deep below the chamber, there rose a low and grinding rumble. The floor began to shake as the dust of a thousand years was stirred from long-forgotten cracks and crevices in the stone overhead. A loud thunk echoed through the chamber as some hidden mechanism dropped into place. Gears and cogs ground away beneath the floor as the stone dais shuddered and slid away from her. The roots digging into the slab contorted, groaned, and snapped, and Malthor's skeleton skittered across the top, then slid off, suspended by the roots as it hung in the air above the newly uncovered opening in the floor.

Stepping forward, Ana held the hilt of her sword out over the chasm. A set of stairs led down into the darkness. She looked up at Malthor's crucified remains, hanging limply from the ceiling.

"Thanks for the sword," she whispered as she stepped down into the opening and disappeared beneath the floor.

13

Ana followed the dusty stairwell in a descending spiral. With her left hand, she braced herself against the central column, while in her right she held Malthor's sword aloft—the gem in its pommel shone a cool white glow across the steps below. Down and down she trod, until at last the stairs leveled out. Here, Ana found a metal gate, beyond which sat a small stone chamber. On the other side of the chamber, a narrow archway was the only other exit.

Ana pushed against the iron bars and found they would not budge. The gate seemed to be locked from the other side. Scanning around the stone frame, she found the hinges were badly rusted. She slipped the sword in between the jamb and the hinge attachment and leaned hard into the heft. With a loud bang, the hinge broke loose, and the gate clattered to the floor in front of her.

Stepping forward, she turned for a moment and looked back toward the stairs. There, on the lintel, an inscription was carved into the stone, but Ana found she could not decipher it. The runes themselves seemed to shift and dance in the light of the sword. She turned back and set off into the narrow tunnel ahead.

As Ana moved farther into the tunnel, she felt a tightness in her chest. The ceiling was just inches above her head, and the walls seemed to close in around her as the darkness threatened to swallow up the light of the sword. She could feel the panic of claustrophobia looming in her bloodstream, filling her veins with the urge to turn back. Looking to her side, she noticed that the walls here were not made of stone at all but of stacks and stacks of bones, packed up against one another like ghoulish cobbles.

She paused for a moment, closed her eyes, and took a deep breath. The air here was wet and stagnant, smelling of dirt and moss. Exhaling through her nose, she opened her eyes, tightened her grip on the sword, and walked forward. Here and there, decrepit skulls grinned out at her as she pressed onward into the catacombs.

After a few more paces, she could start to make out the vague outline of a skeleton, rising out of the darkness ahead of her. Slowing her approach, she raised the hilt to eye level. The sword illuminated the wall to which the skeleton was shackled. She had reached an intersection—the path split here and extended off to her left and right. As she stood and deliberated which way to go, the skeleton's jaw creaked open slightly, and it whispered a chilling "*Hhhaaasssttt …*"

At once Ana's sword was at the ready. She swung forward instinctively. A cloud of dust and bone splinters erupted into the air as the deadly sharp blade embedded itself in the wall behind the skeleton, forging a clean cut through the spine between the ribs and the pelvis. The lower half of the body clattered to the floor, sending echoes down the corridors in every direction.

Ana stood for a moment in silence, panting as she scanned the hallways for any sign of movement. Slowly she leaned in to extricate the sword. It was then that she noticed a curious smoky darkness, flickering almost like a flame, in the skeleton's rib cage. It billowed up and out through the skeleton's mouth, nose, and eye sockets, evaporating into the inky blackness just outside the reach of the sword's light.

"What the hell was that?" Ana whispered. "Where am I?"

As her eyes hunted about for traces of the shadowy flame, she noticed another plaque set into the wall above the skeleton. This inscription, too, was strangely indecipherable to her, as though the letters kept shifting and merging into one another. After a moment or two, however, they settled enough for her to make out a message in the graven stone.

"THE SCRYPTS," it read plainly.

How odd, she thought, her face scrunched up at the effort of reading the ephemeral runes. *Well, it's left or right. Nothing to do but pick one and commit.*

Turning to her left, she held the sword out in front of her once again and set off into the darkness.

*   *   *

For some time, Ana continued through the hallways, winding her way through the bones and always turning left when met with an intersection. Occasionally she would find another inscription or plaque embedded in the wall, but always it would seem scrambled or nonsensical. As she paused in front of one such monument, she breathed in deeply once again and felt her shoulders fall. The tip of the sword came to rest gently on the ground as she stared into the darkness ahead.

"Where am I supposed to go?" she asked no one in particular.

One by one, the letters to her side began to resolve once again.

"GO STRAIGHT, THEN RIGHT, AND CONTINUE THROUGH THE NEXT INTERSECTION."

At this, Ana's mouth sat agape.

"Who are you?" she asked at last.

The text on the wall remained unchanged.

She set off again at a brisk pace. Her right turn took her twisting around through the stacks of bones until she arrived at another intersection. Continuing forward, the hallway opened up slightly into a long, narrow room. The walls here were stone, roughly hewn, like Malthor's chamber above. Deep recesses had been carved into them—three on one side, and three on the other. Each funerary alcove contained human remains, but the bones here were covered in cobwebs and had deteriorated to an almost unrecognizable state. More importantly to Ana, above each alcove, an inscription was carved into the stone, shifting and flickering in the light of the sword.

Six questions, she thought to herself. She took a deep breath and organized her thoughts.

Finally she spoke. "Who are you?"

Her voice echoed in the chamber, but as always, it was met with silence.

As she looked up toward the inscription to her left, it began to resolve: "A FRIEND."

Ana knit her brow. Turning to her right, she held the pommel of her sword up to the next inscription and spoke again. "Why are you helping me?"

"YOU SEEM LOST."

Ana was even less satisfied with this answer than the previous. With two inscriptions committed to the ancient stone, she surmised only four chances remained to get some information from these enchanted walls. Her mind turned to Doro above. Had he managed to wrest himself free from those shambling horrors, or …? Her heart sank at the thought of Doro buried under a mountain of writhing bodies.

"How can I get back to the surface?"

"WHY BOTHER? AMBER ISN'T UP THERE."

At this, Ana was taken aback. How did this entity know Amber's name? Or that Ana was looking for her? Ana's heart began to beat faster, and she turned around to illuminate the inscription above the alcove in the middle of the wall behind her.

"Where is she?"

"YOU KNOW WHERE SHE IS."

At this, Ana reeled back with frustration, squeezing the grip of the sword as she ran her other hand through her hair. Darting back to the opposite wall, she continued her interrogation with a quivering shout. "Tell me where I can find her!"

"I CAN ONLY TELL YOU WHERE TO LOOK."

And with that, Ana had only one opportunity left. She sighed, her heart pounding in her ears as she gazed up toward the darkened ceiling. Once again she breathed in deeply, the moist air smelling of dust and decay.

Looking down again toward the opposite wall, she brought her sword to bear on the final alcove. In it sat a long-forgotten corpse festooned with an elaborate costume. Most of it was tattered and ruined, save for a remarkably well-preserved death mask that shone a pallid yellow in the sword's light. Its lifeless eyes stared up at Ana, and she found herself transfixed by its gaze.

Step by step, Ana drew closer, and she reached out her left hand as if to touch it. Just before she reached the body, her eyes were caught by another set of flickering runes just above the alcove. Here was the last inscription, shifting silently in the dim light of the sword. Its impassive runes faded in and out of Ana's perception, taunting her with the promise of a moment of clarity. Ana closed her eyes.

"How do I get out of here?"

Upon opening her eyes once more, the answer was spelled out before her: "RIGHT, LEFT, RIGHT, UP THE STAIRS. LOOK OUT FOR SPIDERS."

Ana felt her stomach lurch. At once a mess of eyes and mandibles flashed through her mind, and her heartbeat quickened. The silence of the crypt began to swell into a hushed whisper of distant skittering. Holding the sword aloft, she sprinted off into the darkness once more.

*　　*　　*

As Ana reached the top of the stairs, the room opened up into a great black expanse. She could see nothing ahead except for a few stone columns rising up into the darkness above, and a faint glow ahead. She stepped cautiously into the room, holding her sword out in front of her. Step by step, she inched toward the glow on the other side of the room. Eventually, she realized the light was coming from a small crack—the outline of a doorway of some sort.

Now just a few feet from the exit, she stopped suddenly. A sharp crack echoed through the chamber as a drop of liquid hit the ground just in front of her right foot. And then another. And another.

Slowly she crouched down and began to pivot around her right foot. Then, in one fluid movement, she leaped up, thrusting her sword into the darkness just as an enormous black mass of bristling hair lunged down toward her. The blade plunged into the creature's abdomen, spilling out a fetid ichor and drenching Ana's arm. The creature hissed and reeled back, clambering up a thick rope of silk as its pedipalps twitched in agony.

As the sword dislodged from its target, Ana felt a tug on the blade, as if it were urging her off to the left. She turned her head slightly and caught some motion in her peripheral vision. Swinging the blade around, the light caught another huge arachnid as it reared up and swung in with its forelegs. Malthor's sword flickered back and forth in Ana's hand as if it had a mind of its own. Try as she might, however, she could not find purchase on the spider's nimble limbs.

Ana stepped back and began to inch her way toward the door as the spider advanced upon her. In the black recesses of the hall, she could hear the hissing and skittering of yet more reinforcements. Her back now up against a large stone door, she pressed into it with all her weight, but it would not budge.

Stepping to the side, she attempted to skirt the perimeter and draw the creature away from the door. As she drew nearer to the sides of the room, however, the skittering in the darkness grew louder as more and more smaller spiders began to pour down the walls. In front of her, the larger spider strode toward her, striking out with its massive legs and champing at her with its frothing maw.

Ana managed to parry each lunging strike, but her arm was beginning to tire from fending off the incessant attacks of the lumbering beast before her. Shifting her weight around, she swung out at the creature's face, but her reach was insufficient, and the spider now had an opportunity.

It reached out with one of its hulking forelegs and swept Ana's legs out from under her. She hit the floor with a loud thunk but managed to roll out of the way of the spider's razor-sharp chelicerae as they clattered into the stone floor.

Scrambling to her feet, she found herself once again between the great stone door behind her and the slavering behemoth ahead. It sank down in a tight ball and dipped forward, as if preparing to charge. Ana stepped backward and stood in front of the door, lowering her sword. Suddenly the spider's legs launched back and sent the creature flying forward. Ana hit the deck as the creature sailed past her and collided with the door. In a deafening crash, the door swung open, bathing the chamber in blinding daylight.

The spider hissed and shrieked in the light, staggering back and forth as it groped lamely for the doorway. Ana hugged the ground as it lumbered over her and back into the shaded crypt, its eyes robbed of sight by the midday sun. For a moment, Ana lay motionless on the ground, listening to the chittering chorus of clacks and scrapes as the spiders retreated from the room.

After a few more minutes, she braced herself against the stone floor and stood up slowly. She could feel a warm breeze on her skin. The air was once again fresh and vibrant, with notes of sassafras and wildflowers. Turning her back on the tomb, she walked through the doorway and out into a small graveyard set into the base of a hill. As her eyes continued to adjust to the light, the tops of small buildings far in the distance glinted in the sun.

14

Fog was beginning to roll in thick blankets over the small coastal fishing village of Peju. Several miles north and east of the Gyrewood, Peju was the main port by which the denizens of Istabar departed for other lands. The Isle of Hope had several larger ports, the largest of which was south of Harveston, but Peju was the closest to the city and happened to be connected directly by train.

The town was built on a rocky coastline and consisted of a number of small buildings, simple in construction, with tiered, sloping roofs covered in small iridescent shingles that overlapped one another not unlike the scales of a fish. The main thoroughfare featured a semipermanent array of market stalls flanking either side of the street. There was an inn here, a post office, the train station, of course, and some smaller shops and groceries. Fresh catches were always on display.

At the end of the central avenue, where the road stopped and the sea began, was the harbormaster's office. Just past that, standing over the rocks and the water, was a long quay that stretched in both directions down the coastline for some distance. At various intervals, a number of piers jutted off into the water. A handful of small boats were moored here and there. The largest pier, closest to the main street, had a large tower erected at its end, with a stairwell winding up to a platform swaying back and forth gently in the ocean breeze.

As the sun set over the swamp to the west, the fog began to glow a deep red, and row upon row of colored paper lanterns sprang to life along the thoroughfare. Standing at the edge of the pier, looking out across the ocean, Ras Dashen gazed out into the glowing mists.

Slowly at first, then with increasing resolution, a large shape lumbered out of the clouds. It was an enormous jellyfish in the shape of a Portuguese man-of-war, floating down through the sky. Fastened under it was a small gondola, no doubt bringing passengers and goods from the islands to the north. Slowly it floated up to the tower on the pier and lazily wrapped one of its tendrils around a pole atop the boarding spire, while the others dangled down to bob gently in the waves below.

As the patrons began to step out of the gondola and descend from the tower, Ras Dashen turned back to the harbormaster's office, his blue-and-purple robe fluttering back and forth in the chilly air. Walking up to the window, he stood on his tiptoes and placed a bag of coins on the counter with a decisive thud.

"The Isle of Truth," he said. "One way."

A short, stout man who appeared to be mostly fish poked his face out of the window. His head was submerged in what looked like a large diving helmet filled with water. Making some bubbling noises, he grasped the bag of coinage and spilled its contents onto the sill between himself and the cat. He slid each coin from one side of the wooden shelf to the other with his stubby webbed fingers until he was satisfied that the fare had been fully accounted for.

Reaching back into his small booth, he pulled out a ticket and handed it over to the impatient cat, who muttered a thanks and set off back up the road.

Ras Dashen moved at a brisk pace up the street, cloak pulled over his head to hide his face from the handful of men, women, and fish people walking up and down the market stalls. Glancing at the ticket, he saw the departure time was still an hour hence—more time than he wanted to spend out in the open, but it looked like he didn't have much of a choice. As he continued up the street, his eyes darted back and forth into the doorways and shadowy awnings of houses and shops on either side.

Suddenly he stopped dead in his tracks. Two guard dogs were exiting the train station immediately to his right. Pulling the hood of his cloak up to conceal his face further, he spun to the left and slid into the nearest establishment on the opposite side of the street. The large fish-shaped wooden sign out front identified it as the Battered Cod, a tavern of modest renown.

Inside, the atmosphere was dim and dusky. Patrons sat at the bar swilling pints of the local brew, while a handful of tables littered the floor. Ras Dashen crept up to the bar, pulled out a stool, and sidled up next to a large individual that effectively blocked the line of sight between himself and the door.

The bartender, a haggard catfish-like fellow, once again tethered to some sort of breathing device, motioned for an order.

"How about a Singapore Sling?"

The bartender tilted his head in confusion, sending the water in his helmet sloshing back and forth.

"Just pour the beer," said Ras Dashen, sliding a coin across the table. His eyes were trained on the door, ready to jump ship at a moment's notice should Charles's goon squad make an appearance.

"Fancy tastes for a fancy feline, eh?" muttered a rough, gravelly voice. The hackles on Ras Dashen's neck rose up, but he remained motionless atop the stool.

"This feline's had the ale here before and knows better than to ask for it first."

The large man next to Ras Dashen chuckled, coughing as he washed the quip down with another swig from his flagon.

"And what brings a clever cat like you to a backwater bar like this?"

Ras Dashen sat for a moment, eyes still trained on the door, as he considered his response. "A new start," he said at last.

"Mmm … lotsa folks come through Peju looking for a fresh stab at it. The Isle of Hope ain't what it used to be. I hear even Istabar's gone downhill lately."

Ras Dashen sat silently, sipping from his mug.

"Why, I heard that just a couple of days ago, some young lady showed up from who knows where and managed to put a knife through the councillor of the Weavers' Guild. Can you believe that? Threw the whole city into chaos. And her husband, who's supposed to take up the charge, is locked in his room and won't come out."

Ras Dashen eyed the stranger with an icy stare.

"Now, why do you think he's taking so long to put the Weavers' Guild to rights?"

"He must be bereft at the loss of his wife," whispered the cat through gritted teeth.

One hand still affixed to the flagon in front of him, the stranger moved his cloak back slightly, revealing a dagger. The blade was neatly gilded with an elaborate needle-and-thread motif. His tone changed abruptly and he lowered his voice.

"Cut the crap, Ras. You and I both know you're not leaving this shithole on your own two legs. Either you come quiet with me right now, or Charles's dogs walk in through that door and chain you to a rock on the Isle of Fear for the rest of your short, miserable life. Frankly, I don't care either way, but there's at least a chance Lord Various will kill you quickly if you tell him what he wants to know."

"How charitable of you to offer Ras Dashen a choice in the manner of his death."

"Well, it doesn't have to be that way, now, does it? You can give it to me right now, and I can walk out of this place easy-peasy."

"Give what to you?"

"Don't play dumb with me, cat. If you have the Signet, hand it over. If you sold it—and I can't believe even *you* would be dumb enough to sell it—but if you don't have it on you, then you're coming with me, and you're probably dead by tomorrow."

The cat's eyes widened. "Ras Dashen does not know what you're talking about."

The stranger sighed, setting his beer down and slowly standing up from his seat at the bar.

"You messed up, Ras. You had the perfect patsy on your hands, but you got greedy. You took a life, *and* you took the Signet. Now I've got to come out here and tie up loose ends. And if there's anything the Weavers' Guild is good at, it's tying up loose ends."

The dagger flashed out and whistled through the air, slicing through the space occupied by Ras Dashen only a split second before. The cat was in the air, vaulting backward over the stool. He landed, deftly, and slung his cloak out over his arm, whipping it into a long, twisted rope. The stranger threw the stool aside and lunged once again. Ras Dashen dodged to the side and slung the knotted cloak over his assailant's arm, pulling back and wresting the dagger from his hand. It went flying and clattered to the floor.

"Get over here, you little bastard!" The Weavers' Guild thug attempted to reel in the cloak, but his prey had already wriggled out of the tangled fabric.

"Ras Dashen doesn't have your goddamned pin!" The cat dashed under chairs and tables, sprinting on all fours toward the door. The bar was now fully aware of the brawl and had erupted into chaos. Patrons jumped up from their chairs as the stranger charged through, overturning tables and swinging at the feline darting back and forth across the floor. As Ras Dashen bolted for the door, it burst open, revealing two heavily armored canine guards, roused by the uproar.

"What's going on in here?" asked a surly golden retriever.

Ras Dashen slid across the floor and pivoted sharply toward the wall as smaller fights broke out around the dining room. Leaping up from the ground and curling into a tiny ball, he smashed through one of the tavern's windows and landed in a sprinkling of dust and shattered sea glass on the street outside. Turning the corner, he sprinted down an alleyway and then, sprouting devilishly sharp claws, clambered up a drainpipe and began to skitter across the scaly roof.

From rooftop to rooftop, he jumped, trying to put as much distance as possible between himself and the Battered Cod. Heading at breakneck pace, he dived down into an alleyway behind the harbormaster's office and pinned himself against the back of the building, panting heavily. He glanced up to a clock tower on a building several houses down. 8:35. If he could make it another twenty-five minutes, he could wave goodbye to the Isle of Hope forever.

Peering around the corner of the building, he could see several dogs marching down the main drag, noses in the air, filtering off into corners and searching methodically for their prey. At the same time, he knew that the Weavers' Guild thugs were hot on his trail, likely combing the outer regions of the town first and working their way in.

8:37.

He slid around to the opposite end of the rear wall of the building and cast his eyes down the pier toward the tower. The giant man-of-war was still attached to it, floating lazily in the now-inky-black sky. Passengers were beginning to queue up at the base of the spire, and the crew were loading up baggage. Halfway along the pier was a pile of barrels, no doubt filled with the same swill being served up at the Battered Cod, but perhaps it could provide enough cover for a few moments prior to boarding. If he could make it to 8:50, he could make a run for it and jump aboard at last call.

Anxiously he stood, back against the wall of the harbormaster's office, shaking with adrenaline, eyes darting back and forth between the living blimp, the clock tower, and the shadowed alleyways before him. As the clock's minute hand ticked nearer and nearer to the *X*, he steeled his nerves and crouched down for a final sprint. Inching toward the edge of the building, he held his breath and waited for the dogs patrolling up the street to turn a blind eye to the pier.

Three … two … one—

Ras Dashen's vision went black as a hand wrapped around his eyes and mouth. His muffled screams were muted by the pressure of a deathly sharp blade against his throat. He felt himself being pulled backward into the darkness. His body went limp as the smooth cobblestones slid under his paws, moving him farter and farter away from the pier.

His terror gave way to tears as the departure bell tolled in the distance.

15

Ras Dashen opened his eyes.

The only illumination was the pale streetlight oozing through a single window to his right. It looked out into an unremarkable alleyway. Looking down at the wall in front of him, he saw the dim outline of a door. The room was otherwise pitch-black and unremarkable.

He made to move his arm up to quiet a pounding headache and quickly realized that both his arms were completely immobilized. Indeed, his arms and legs had both been tied to a simple chair with scraps of what looked like fabric. Glancing back to the window, he could now see that a curtain had been removed and torn up to fashion the makeshift restraints.

At some point, he reasoned, he must've passed out. As his senses returned to him, he could taste the musty fabric in his mouth, silencing any call for help. Suddenly he became aware of a presence behind him, shuffling about quietly. Checking up on the premises, perhaps, or preparing instruments best suited to the task of knowledge extraction. The henchmen of the Weavers' Guild were known for their creativity—and their results.

The footsteps drew nearer now—quietly—and he felt a tug at the back of his neck. The knot of his gag was slowly being untied. Before it came loose, however, a familiar blade returned to his throat, making clear the price of an attempt at drawing attention to his predicament. The edge pressed urgently against his larynx—even through his fur, he could feel the deadly sharpness of the instrument. As the cloth was pulled free from his mouth, he coughed and spat in indignation. The blade pulled in closer, forcing his chin up, suggesting in no uncertain terms that further conversation was not Ras Dashen's to initiate.

He felt the ebb and flow of soft breath against his left ear as his captor leaned in and stated, in a whisper, "I've been looking for you."

The blood drained out of Ras Dashen's face, and he was hit with a deep, nauseating pang of dread at the cool feminine voice behind him. His paws began to shake uncontrollably even as they remained tied behind his back.

"You did something bad, Ras," she whispered, leaning around to his right side. "The City Guard thinks you're an accomplice to a horrible crime. The Weavers' Guild thinks you've stolen an immeasurably valuable artifact." She stepped around the front now, still brandishing the point of the blade at his throat, silhouetted by the dreary window behind her.

"But I know the truth." She leaned in, and the pressure of the blade grew ever higher. "You're a murderer."

Now that she was directly in front of him and lit by the dying streetlights, Ras Dashen could clearly see Ana's face. Her hair was disheveled, and her countenance smeared with dirt, but there was no mistaking the fierce dedication in her eyes.

"I need to get back into the city, and you're going to help me. The Ruling Council of Istabar needs to know that I had nothing to do with Lady Sundry's death."

"What do you want Ras Dashen to do? Turn himself in?" He scowled, then winced as the sword dug farther into his pelt.

"Ras Dashen will confess to his crime and explain that I am innocent."

"You might as well kill Ras Dashen right now, then," he said, "since it seems like he dies either way. Ras Dashen owes you nothing."

Ana frowned. As a fugitive from justice, she couldn't turn him over to the City Guard directly. If she set him loose and he got caught, chances were he would defend his innocence as a longtime merchant and give up her location in the process.

"Why did you kill Lady Sundry?"

"Because that was what Ras Dashen was paid to do."

"Who paid you?"

Ras Dashen sat in silence.

"Who paid you?" she asked again, barely maintaining her hushed tone. She dug the sword deeper into his neck, and a small trickle of blood began to run down the edge of the blade.

"Ras Dashen does not know," he whispered, his voice quavering in the darkness.

"Who was it?" Ana leaned in closer and bared her teeth.

Ras Dashen's eyes were wet. He began to shiver. "Ras Dashen does not know! He does not know!"

Ana sighed and drew the sword back from his neck and slid it silently into the gilded sheath at her hip. Reaching down, she picked up the makeshift gag and pressed it to Ras Dashen's neck, stanching the small cut. She tied it around in a small bandage and began to untie his feet.

"What ... what are you doing?"

"Getting us out of here," said Ana.

Unraveling the fabric from his feet, she affixed one end to his bound hands and wrapped the other around her hand. She picked him up out of the chair by the scruff of his neck and planted him firmly on his feet. Pushing open the door, she stepped out into the alleyway and yanked firmly on Ras Dashen's leash, pulling him out into the light. Blinking wildly, he rushed to catch up to her brisk pace.

Several corners later, they arrived back at the rear of the harbormaster's building. She peered around the corner toward the dock—the thick fog now obscured all but the nearest pier. Stepping around the front, she walked straight into two large Newfoundlands in helmets and tabards bearing the crest of the City Guard.

"Excuse us, ma'am," began one of the dogs, before the sudden realization of Ana's captive feline's identity set in.

"Is that Ras Dashen?" inquired the other, casting a bewildered gaze down at the diminutive cat, bound in tattered rags. "And you … aren't you Ana? The woman from Seattle?"

"Yes," said Ana with a sigh. "I suppose you've been looking for us."

"Indeed we have been, Miss Ana," replied the guard on the right. "Or at any rate, we were looking for the cat. *You*, we were told, had been moved to the tower. I'm not sure how you escaped, but you will also be joining us on our return trip to Istabar."

At this, Ana was taken aback. How could they not know she had escaped?

"Theodore, if you wouldn't mind?" The dog on the left stepped forward with a nod and produced a pair of manacles. "I'm afraid you're under arrest … again," said the Newfoundland.

Ana shuddered as the cold metal connected around her wrists.

Ras Dashen's fabric bindings were likewise removed and replaced with the iron equivalents. Ana's sword was confiscated, and the two were then led up the street between the two canines until they arrived at the train station.

On the platform, a large steam locomotive sat fuming, waiting for its final evening trip. Stepping aboard,

Ana noted the fine fabrics on the seats, bearing the subtle touch of the Weavers' Guild. The engine and the frames of the cars, however, bore the proud insignia of the Anvil. Walking back into the rear of the car, the guards were happy to let Ana have some space. Ras Dashen, however, was seated snugly in between the two dogs.

After a few minutes, the doors slid shut, and the whistle blew as the train pulled slowly out of the station. As the engine chugged away, the train began to pick up speed. Ana gazed out the windows into the darkness beyond. To the right, there was only endless ocean. It seemed the train ran along the coastline as it made its return to the west. Peering out to the left, she could see the thickening stands of trees and murky water as the outer edge of the Gyrewood pulled into view. In the distance, she could almost make out the lone oak tree atop Malthor's Mound, rising over the center of the swamp.

Ana's heart sank—she thought of the wretched Accursed, and of Doro. Had he made it out of the Gyrewood in one piece? Or had those awful creatures torn him apart, as they had poor Cromag and Gorthek? As the swamp receded into the distant night, she found herself thinking back to the sea cave on the edge of the Midnight Beach. When this was all over, perhaps she could return there and find Doro, watching over the waves from his promontory over the sand.

After some time, the train ducked into a tunnel, and there was nothing further to see outside. She gazed back at the guards, and at Ras Dashen, who seemed awake but quite distant, as though he was still wandering through the daze of his capture. The click-clack of the train as it chugged down the tracks was strangely soothing to Ana, and for the first time in several days, she was reminded of the feeling of sleep.

A sonorous whine echoed through the tunnel as the train began to apply its brakes. A short blast of the horn indicated its last stop was imminent. The tunnel opened up into an opulent underground platform, with sculpted white stone columns in the familiar yet minimal Istabar mode.

Slowly the train ground to a halt, and the doors slid open. The guards rose from their seat and pulled Ras Dashen up with them, ushering him along as he gazed at the floor.

"This way, please," one of the guards called to Ana. She obliged, following them out onto the platform, then up a set of winding stairs to an archway that opened out into the streets above.

The four of them wound back and forth through the labyrinthine passageways, lit by the enchanting hues of the string lights above.

At last they arrived back at the prison. Walking through the gatehouse, they made their way through several sets of doors, each more formidable than the last, until at last they emerged into the prison yard.

"Take this one downstairs, and see to it that he's got food and water. I suspect Charles will want to see him tomorrow."

The other dog took Ras Dashen gently by the shoulder and led him down the stairs to the dungeons below.

The remaining guard turned back to Ana. "You, I think, we need to be a bit more careful with. Come with me."

The two departed back through the first gatehouse door and then turned right, moving through the inside of the structure. They crossed over to the other side of the wall and then began to move up a number of stairs, back and forth, until eventually they reached a door at the top. The guard produced a prodigious key ring and unlocked the large wooden door, gesturing inside.

"Welcome back to the tower. I trust this time, you'll behave yourself. We can't have you disappearing before the trial."

Ana stepped through the door, and the guard stepped in behind her. A lock clicked in her cuffs and they fell away. She took her wrists in her hands and turned to see the door being shut behind her. "Good night," said the guard from behind the door as it clicked shut, "and try to get some rest."

His footsteps died away as he padded back down the stairs.

Ana stood in a small but well-appointed room. There was a bed here—not a cot but a real bed, with sheets and a pillow. A small end table held a glass of water and a handful of books. The windows were barred, but as she crossed the room and looked out, they afforded a beautiful view of the world beyond the city walls—over the waterfall below and out into the ocean. And to her surprise, there was a separate bathroom, with a toilet, a shower, a sink, and a mirror. Standing in front of the mirror, in the light of a candle burning gently in the room, she saw for the first time her dirt-smeared face staring back at her.

Turning on the faucet, she splashed her face and scrubbed it as best she could. As the water dripped down off her hair and her eyelashes, the depth of her exhaustion settled in on her weary eyes. Pressing a towel to her face, she wandered back into the small bedroom and flopped onto the bed.

As uncertain as she was about her fate in the coming days, for a moment, she felt deeply comforted by the simple linens. As a distant clock tower began to strike midnight, Ana's room dissolved into the warm embrace of sleep.

16

Despite the modern front desk and attractive lobby, the exam room was sterile and uninviting. Generic still lifes and incomprehensible geometric abstractions sat framed on the walls, probably as an afterthought from whatever design firm had been granted the unfortunate task of cheering up a charnel house.

The outpatient facility had a deal with the local oncology department that enabled them to deliver chemotherapy for patients, saving them a trip to the hospital, which was quite a bit farther away. Ana sat on an uncomfortable metal stool while she held Amber's hand. Amber was seated next to her in a cushioned treatment chair, reading a book while clear fluid dripped slowly into her bloodstream. In the hallway, a constant drone of unanswered calls and blaring fax noises drowned out the steady blips of Amber's heart rate monitor.

Periodically a nurse would wander into the room, check the infusion rate, and wander off wordlessly. Ana would look up from her phone, expecting to engage in some sort of human interaction, and then resign herself to simply watching the ritual unfold, again and again. Amber, for her part, was far more interested in her book than the roller-clamp position.

In a quiet moment after one such intrusion, Ana set her phone down in her lap and squeezed Amber's hand. Amber looked up from her book inquisitively.

"Do you think you're going to want to go to Julia's dinner party tomorrow?" asked Ana.

"I'm not sure how I'm going to feel after this. But I have a hard time imagining a world in which I do not want to go to a dinner party." Amber smiled, absentmindedly rubbing her arm.

"Do you ever notice we basically only ever talk about food?"

"But food is so good." Amber gazed wistfully off into space.

"Did the doctor say how many of these you need to do?"

"She said they're going to do a repeat scan after the first one, and then they'll decide how many more after that," said Amber.

Ana patted her hand gently. "Well, you're doing great."

"Yeah, sitting in a chair is really hard. I've been practicing pretty much all my life for this moment."

Ana rolled her eyes and went back to scrolling through Instagram.

*　　*　　*

As the sun rose over Istabar, golden light crept through the windows of Ana's tower room. Turning over to shield her eyes from the glow, she heard a knock at the door. She pushed the sheets aside, then slid out of bed and padded barefoot over the wooden floor to peer out through the small barred window in the door. On the other side stood a large, stocky Bernese mountain dog in an emerald-green robe. The dog smiled in the way that dogs do, turning the corners of her jowls up and squinting slightly.

"Good morning," she said. "My name is Nora; I'm an adjutant to Captain Charles. He asked me to inform you that you'll be taken to trial today." She bent down and unlatched a small aperture at the bottom of the door. It was a smaller door, the size of a bread box, perhaps, and she pushed through it a metal tray. On the left side of the tray sat a pair of sandals, a rope belt, and a few bronze pins featuring the aegis of the City Guard. On the right, there was a neatly folded cloth garment, on top of which had been placed a plate heaping with eggs, bacon, and buttered toast.

"I've brought a fresh change of clothes for you, and some breakfast. I'll be back in thirty minutes to take you to the Tower of Drasz, where you will plead your case for innocence in front of the council."

"Do I get a lawyer?" asked Ana.

"In Istabar, defendants represent themselves," said Nora. "There will be a call for testimony at the discretion of each councillor. We will lay out the facts as best we can establish them, and then you will plead your case. The trial will be decided by a majority vote of the council members present."

"Will Ras Dashen be there?"

"I cannot speak to the witnesses selected by the council members, but I would be surprised if he was not."

Nora turned and walked back down the hallway, rounding the corner and descending the many steps back to the gatehouse. Ana bent down to retrieve the tray and cross the room back to her bed. She placed the plate on her nightstand and arrayed the clothing atop the sheets. Taking the plate in hand, she ate in quiet contemplation, imagining the trial ahead. Would she have the opportunity to confront Ras Dashen directly? What would he say in his defense? What sort of surprise witnesses lay in wait for her on behalf of the other heads of the guilds of Istabar?

After a quick shower, she donned the clothing provided to her by Nora. It was after the fashion of much of the garb she had seen so far in the city: a simple chiton that could be pinned about the shoulders, and hung loosely down to the calves. She tied the belt around her waist and smoothed out the fabric. It was of simple design, a vivid sky blue fringed with a sort of arabesque pattern.

After slipping on the sandals, she waited by the window for Nora's return.

Outside, the city of Istabar was waking up, setting up market stalls and rolling out colorful banners. Glimmering streams of crystal-clear water painted shimmering rainbows on the blanched white walls of the buildings as they cascaded from innumerable small channels and aqueducts. Vibrant green ivy crawled down distant facades as fruit-laden trees reached up to meet them.

It really is a beautiful city, thought Ana. *I wonder if I'll ever get to walk its streets again.*

*   *   *

"This is outrageous!" Various paced about the small council chamber. "As duly elected councillor of the Weavers, I cannot be refused a role in the adjudication of this trial."

"I must remind you, Lord Various, that until you bear the Signet of the Weavers, you are an esteemed guest in this chamber, but you are not a councillor," said Persephone, her voice soft but firm. "And we are happy to continue with the confirmation as soon as you are ready to take up that duty. But even if you do so this very morning, it is the opinion of this council that your participation in the adjudication of this case would constitute a conflict of interest. Surely you can agree that you may have difficulty in maintaining impartiality around the matter of Lady Sundry's death."

"With all due respect, Councillor, I believe it is my right

as councillor-elect to have some say in the matter of my wife's brutal murder at the hands of this outsider."

"And so you shall," said Lord Drasz, "for as the only other known occupant of that box, you will be called as a witness to testify to your experience."

"Don't worry, Various," said Olen. "Justice will be served this day. We'll get to the bottom of this heinous crime. Lady Sundry's murderer will pay for what they've done."

Various crossed his arms, frustration writ large across his furrowed brow. "Very well," he said at last. "I thank the council for their diligence in this matter, and I trust that their judgment will be swift and decisive. The people of Istabar are depending on it."

With that, he turned and descended the spiraling stairs out of the chamber.

Benjamin turned to address his compatriots. "That went about as well as I expected," he said with a sigh.

"My heart bleeds for the poor man," said Persephone. "He lost his wife a week ago now, and her killer remains free from accountability for this reprehensible act. He yearns for justice."

"We cannot simply execute someone based on the word of one man, bereaved though he may be," said Charles. "Much as I would like this to be over and done with, the accused has just as much a right to due process as does anyone else."

"Of course you are right, my dear Charles," said Persephone, "but you must admit, it's not much of a case. She was the only other person in the box that night, as attested to by Lord Various and your own guards."

"The knife had to come from somewhere. She did not enter the opera with it," said Charles.

"Well, either way, we're not going to decide it here in this room," said Olen as he stood from his chair. "I'll see ye all downstairs in a few. I've got to go organize my witnesses."

"Agreed," said Benjamin. "And I suggest the rest of us do the same."

* * *

Bounding down the street, carrying a basket overflowing with groceries from the market, a tiny Bernese puppy spun around to look for her father. The large black dog with a broad farmer's hat stepped out from behind a stall, hefting a sack of potatoes.

"Wait for me, love! I'm coming!"

She hopped up and down impatiently, waiting for her father to catch up. As he trundled up to her, she turned and resumed her skip down the road toward the main drag.

As she neared the grand thoroughfare, her progress was arrested by a sizable crowd blocking the way. She hopped up and down, trying to get a view of the spectacle ahead. Coming up behind her, her father gently heaved the sack of potatoes down to the ground and scooped his daughter up, placing her atop his wide-brimmed straw hat so she could see over the gathered throng.

"See anyone you know?" he asked. The crowd was strangely quiet for how many people had gathered to witness the event. Walking up the street, flanked on either side by hulking armored pit bulls, were two individuals.

"It's Mama!" the tiny pup cried out in delight. She pointed to the black-coated dog in green robes walking beside a young woman in light blue. "What's she doing?"

"She's taking that young woman to the tower," said her father. "They're going to have the trial today."

"Can we go and watch?"

"No, my dear. We have to go to work today! But I'm sure your mother will tell you all about it when she gets home tonight."

The precocious pup sat and watched with wide-eyed curiosity as the entourage turned down the central avenue and out of sight.

17

The Tower of Drasz was comprised of many floors, each serving a separate function in the governance of Istabar. At the top sat the council chamber, a room few citizens were ever given the opportunity to behold in person. Below that were actuarial offices, accounting facilities, and other such affairs relevant to the Bank of Drasz. Intermingled with and below these lofty positions were various bureaus dedicated to the component of each guild that dealt most closely with the administration of the city—the Anvil oversaw civil infrastructure here; the Farmers had an office for the licensure of market stalls; and even the City Guard maintained a department for policy around law enforcement.

At the base of the tower was a grand courtroom, cylindrical in shape. It sat just beyond the entryway and stood as silent testimony to the depth of Drasz's coffers. The theme of delicate channels and fountains that featured prominently in Istabar's streets continued into the court as shimmering sheets of water poured down and collected in a basin below the room. Tall, thin rectangular windows let in the light from above, casting broad rays of immaculate sunbeams down into the chamber and shimmering into the waters below.

The entry area opened onto a platform suspended over the water, held by cables anchored to the walls and ceiling. It hung in the center as a broad circle surrounded by shimmering waters and glowing sunlight. At the head of the room, opposite the entryway, a balcony opened out into the chamber. Upon this balcony sat five chairs, emblazoned with the same five symbols carved into the stones, woven into the tapestries, baked into the breads, forged into the weaponry, and stamped onto the coins throughout the city. On either side of this main balcony, two smaller openings in the wall were fitted with chairs and desks.

All around the other side of the room, above the entryway, were arranged a number of balconies, now filling up with the citizens of Istabar who had come to witness what promised to be the trial of the century. A swift silence fell over the bustle and murmur of the congregation as the water curtain parted and two burly guards stood at the edge of the entryway.

Accompanied by a Bernese mountain dog in an emerald-green robe, a young woman walked confidently across the threshold and up onto the platform. Her hands were bound behind her, but her eyes were fierce and determined. She strode up to the center of the platform and stood firmly. The dog took up a position a few feet behind.

The silence in the room was deafening. The gentle hush of falling water echoed throughout the chamber, uninterrupted by even a whisper from the audience. One by one, the venerable council members shuffled into position on their balcony above the platform. Persephone first, in the rightmost position, then Benjamin in the center, Charles and Olen on the left. The chair between Benjamin and Persephone, embellished with a delicate needle and thread, was notably empty.

In unison, the councillors took their seats, all except Benjamin. Smashing through the silence at last, the booming voice of Lord Benjamin Drasz filled the chamber.

"Citizens of the great city of Istabar, we gather here today to adjudicate the matter of the death of Lady Sundry Quinn, Head of the Weavers' Guild and member of the Ruling Council of Istabar. Before you stands the accused, Miss Ana, heritage unknown. I now invite Lady Persephone of the Farmers' Guild to detail the accusations against this woman."

Benjamin took a seat, and Persephone stood to address the courtroom.

"The council has reason to believe you were involved in the murder of Lady Sundry Quinn. If found to be an accessory to this event, you face a maximum sentence of life imprisonment. If found to be the executor of this event, you face a commensurate sentence of death."

A quiet gasp filtered through the audience. Such a punishment was nigh unheard of in the modern era.

"Captain Charles of the City Guard has been leading the investigation of this case. Captain Charles, would you kindly lay out the facts as you know them?"

Charles stood and cleared his throat.

"On the second day of the week, in the week preceding this trial, Lady Sundry Quinn was murdered. The event took place during a performance at the opera house. At the close of the first act, Lady Sundry Quinn was found dead with a dagger in her chest. She was seated in a box, in the immediate company of Lord Various Quinn and the accused.

"No other individuals are known to have entered or exited the box during the performance other than two guards posted outside, who removed the body of Lady Sundry and escorted the accused to the prison."

"It was Ras Dashen," said Ana. "He came into the box and stabbed Lady Sundry as the lights went out."

"You will be silent until it is your turn to speak," said Benjamin. "If you interrupt these proceedings again, I will hold you in contempt."

Ana glared back as Benjamin gestured for Charles to continue.

"The Guard has questioned a number of individuals with respect to this case. While we have not uncovered the presence of any other individuals in the box that night, we also have not yet been able to determine how the knife arrived at the theater. It is the opinion of this councillor that we open the floor to witness testimony so that we may corroborate or invalidate Ana's assertion of innocence."

"Very well," said Benjamin. "Then I would like to proceed with our first witness."

Charles nodded. "I call to the stand Mr. Dusty Barnes, general manager of the Istabar Opera."

Out from the balcony to the right of the councillors came a large black dog in a grey-blue cloak. His face was gentle and wizened, and he smiled down at the young woman on the platform below him.

"Mr. Barnes," Charles began. "Were you there on the night this event occurred?"

"I was," said the old dog.

"And you saw the accused enter the theater?"

"I did."

"And she proceeded through the security checkpoint with the rest of the patrons?"

"Indeed she did."

From a table to his right, Charles produced a wicked-looking dagger. It was plain in its construction, almost unremarkable, but its blade was barbed in a way that ensured a one-way trip through its target. Once in, it would not be removed without mortally wounding its victim.

"Did you find this dagger on her person as she entered the opera?"

"I did not, sir."

"Did you find it on anyone else entering the building that day?"

"No, sir."

"How else might this weapon have made its way into the building if not carried by a patron through the front door?"

"I don't know, sir. It is possible someone entered the theater by nontraditional means, through a window or another access. But while we make every effort to ensure the safety and security of our patrons, we cannot monitor every crack and crevice in our aging building."

Charles nodded. "I understand. Thank you, Mr. Barnes."

Dusty headed back into the gallery behind the balcony, and Charles continued with the proceedings.

"For our second witness, I defer to Carver Olen."

The stout councillor stood and approached the banister, addressing the gathered crowd. "Thank ye, Captain. I call to the stand Mr. Ian Woon."

Ian Woon was a wiry fellow. He wore a blacksmith's smock and heavy gloves, even to his appearance in the illustrious High Court of Istabar.

"Mr. Woon, ye are the man who crafted this dagger, are ye not?"

"Yes, milord," said Ian.

Olen walked over to the side of the balcony and gestured at a small engraving at the base of the blade, holding it out for Ian's inspection.

"Is this yer maker's mark here, just above the hilt?"

Ian craned his neck over the waters below, squinting to make out the small figures along the side of the blade.

"It is, milord."

"And to whom did ye sell this weapon?"

"I will have to check my ledger," he said, producing a large leather-bound book. He opened the book and began to pore over its contents, mouthing various names and numbers as he searched, page by page, back into the recent past.

"Ah," he said at last. "Here, nine weeks ago. This dagger's number was registered to one Amber of Seattle."

Ana gasped. Amber had been in Istabar after all. And she had bought this dagger—which meant she might have even met Ras Dashen.

"And who is this Amber of Seattle?" Olen continued.

"A traveler through our city, milord. I know not where she is now."

Olen drummed his fingers against the balcony, staring down at the blade in his hands.

"Very well. Thank ye for yer testimony."

As Olen returned to his seat, Charles rose again.

"For our third witness, I call to the stand Mr. Ras Dashen."

Two guards appeared on the balcony, flanking a diminutive feline, his hands clasped behind his back.

"Mr. Dashen, you have been implicated by the accused in this crime. Would you please inform us of your whereabouts on the evening of the incident?"

Ras Dashen approached the edge of the balcony and looked over it, down upon Ana. She met his gaze and returned an icy glare.

"Ras Dashen … Ras Dashen was in the market district, packing for departure to Harveston."

"Liar!" Ana cried. "You liar! You came into the box and thrust that knife through Lady Sundry's heart, you villainous monster!"

"Enough!" bellowed Benjamin. "If you interrupt these proceedings again, you will be taken back to the prison, and we will deliberate without your input."

Ana stood fuming as the cat continued.

"Ras Dashen was packing goods into his carts, preparing for the trip to Harveston on the next day."

"Where did you sleep that night?" asked Charles.

"In one of the carts," he said, staring at the ground.

"And is there anyone who can corroborate your presence in the market district all evening?"

"You can ask any of Ras Dashen's caravan. They were all there with Ras Dashen."

"Hmm," mumbled Charles. "Very well. I would like to open the floor to the accused. Ana, would you tell the court, in your own words, what happened that evening?"

Ras Dashen began to back away from the balcony but was stopped in his tracks by a sharp look from Charles.

"Mr. Dashen, I have not yet dismissed you."

Ana cleared her throat, looking up at Benjamin, who nodded his head curtly in approval.

"I entered the opera house alone and proceeded up the stairs to the box assigned to the Weavers' Guild. Lord Various and Lady Sundry joined me shortly thereafter, and the opera began. Toward the end of the first act, my attention was drawn to the door behind us, which had opened slightly. That's when I saw Ras Dashen in a black robe leap up behind

Lady Sundry's chair. Under the cover of the noise onstage, he stabbed her in the chest and ran out through the door. How he evaded your guards on the other side, I do not know. But when the lights came up, Lady Sundry was dead."

"Is this true?" said Charles, looking back toward Ras Dashen.

"Ras Dashen would never do such a thing."

"Look me in the eye, Ras."

"Charles." Benjamin's stern voice carried with it an air of admonition.

Ras Dashen's gaze slowly crept up until it met with Charles's steely glare. The seconds crept by in excruciating tension.

"Alright, thank you, Mr. Dashen," said Charles at last. The cat disappeared from the balcony, and the canine took his seat once again.

"Thank you, Captain Charles," said Benjamin. "For the final witness, I call to the stand Lord Various Quinn, councillor-elect of the Weavers' Guild."

This announcement elicited a gasp of surprise from the audience. From the balcony to the right of the platform, Various emerged, bedecked in the black garb of mourning, silvery-white hair glinting in an errant sunbeam. Nervous whispers spread like wildfire through the gathered throng. He stood on the precipice of the balcony, hands on the railing, staring down at Ana.

"Lord Various, thank you for joining us. The court recognizes that this is a difficult time for you, and your testimony in this case is appreciated."

"I will do whatever I can to bring my wife's killer to justice." His voice was quiet, but his tone revealed a deep anguish. Ana couldn't help but feel the weight of his sorrow in her own chest as he took the stand.

"Would you recount for us your experience that evening, in as much detail as you can?"

"Certainly. My dear Lady Sundry and I entered the box with this woman prior to the beginning of the opera. Lady Sundry took a seat next to the accused, and I sat on her other side. At the close of the act, there was a scream onstage, and then the lights plunged us into darkness. When they came back up, my wife lay dead, pinned to her chair by that dagger. No one else entered or left the box during that time."

"I see. Do you recall blood on this woman's hands?"

"I do not remember." Various's voice began to tremble. "I pulled the dagger from her body, but she was already dead. There was so much blood."

"It's alright. Thank you, Lord Various."

Various turned away from the audience but then paused and turned back for a moment, looking out over the courtroom.

"Lady Sundry brought a kind of joy to my life that I suspect I will never rekindle. Justice this day will not bring her back, but it may begin to heal the hole left gaping in all our hearts."

As Various stepped out into the darkness beyond the balcony, Benjamin nodded sagely in agreement. Ana stifled a wave of nausea as Various's words played over and over again in her mind. Everyone seemed to be staring at her, weighing her worth against the tragedy of a broken man.

"Very well," said Benjamin. "We have heard the testimony from all individuals deemed necessary for the successful prosecution of this case. If there are no further items, this court will recess for thirty minutes while the council deliberates, after which we will render our verdict."

The councillors stood and, one by one, filtered out of the room. The din of various conversations surged into the open space as the audience began to speculate on which way the case would go.

"What happens now?" Ana asked, turning to Nora.

"Now we wait."

18

As the council members returned to their seats, a hush fell upon the audience once again. Ana stood defiantly in the center of the chamber.

Rising from his chair, Benjamin addressed the courtroom once again. "After a great deal of deliberation, we have come to a decision. The council is split, two in favor of charging the accused with the offense of the premeditated murder of Lady Sundry Quinn. The other two favor the declaration of a mistrial and subsequent reopening of the investigation. Given that one of our members is missing, it is the opinion of this court that we gather the recommendation of councillor-elect Lord Various Quinn following a personal inquiry with the accused. Ana will report to Lord Various's office this evening, and the council will reconvene with Lord Various's report in hand tomorrow morning to deliver the final verdict."

Benjamin picked up a small gavel from the armrest of his chair and rapped it soundly on the wood. The assembled throng began to rise and shuffle out of the room as the councillors did the same. Ana and Nora were left on the platform alone.

"What happens now?" asked Ana, turning to the canine adjutant.

"Now we return you to the prison, I'm afraid. It seems the council has offered you a chance to discuss your case directly with your accuser. In the meanwhile, we will continue to cross-examine Ras Dashen. I don't think Captain Charles is entirely convinced of his alibi."

As Ana turned and made her way out of the courtroom, she paused to look back at the now-empty room. From the balcony to the right of the councillors' seats, she could almost see someone gazing back at her from the darkness.

*   *   *

That night, it was not Nora who came to Ana's lofty cell, but Captain Charles. He knocked on her door softly.

"Come in," she said, crossing the wooden floor to present her wrists. To her surprise, he unlocked the door and swung it wide open. Walking into the room, he shut the door behind him, but it remained unlocked.

"Miss Ana, I must apologize for putting you through all of this. I know how frustrating it must be to have this ordeal standing in the way of your search for your friend, but I believe we may yet have a chance to prove your innocence."

Ana, surprised at such trust from the stout canine, stepped back and took a seat on the bed.

"What do you suggest? Right now, it's just my word against Ras Dashen's, and he's been here a lot longer than I have."

"Justice for Lady Sundry's murder is not the only thing at stake in this trial," said Charles, lowering his voice. "When we first took you in, you had something on your person. An item you shouldn't have had."

"The Signet?"

"Indeed. But I happen to know that Lady Sundry wasn't wearing the Signet that evening. She told me she had given it to someone for safekeeping just before the council meeting earlier that day. I do not think it is a coincidence that you now bear the Signet. I think she chose you for a reason. That is why the prison's secret passageways to the outside world were somewhat less secret than usual the night of your escape—which, by the way, is still a matter of confidence between you, me, and the two guards you so expertly wandered into in Peju."

Charles winked as Ana began to realize his role in her earlier flight from the city.

"Lord Various misses his wife, but I suspect he is also searching for the Signet. He has already come to the prison to interrogate Ras Dashen, to no avail, but I think it has strengthened the possibility in his mind that Ras Dashen was involved. I think he believes it was stolen from Lady Sundry that night, and that by finding the Signet, he will find Lady Sundry's killer as well. It was my hope that your escape would buy us the time we needed to track down Ras Dashen and get a confession out of him. But since you are now here as well, time is no longer on our side.

"We may still have a chance, however. Tonight, when you meet Lord Various, tell him how you came to possess the Sirens' Silk. He may see this as a sign of good faith and characterize you favorably in his recommendation. And whatever you do, don't mention the Signet. In fact, it would be best if you left it with me. We may need it in the trials to come."

"But I can't give you the Signet." Ana wrung her hands in her lap as she gazed down toward the floor. "I don't have it anymore."

Charles's eyes widened. "Who does?"

"No one. I lost it in the Gyrewood."

Charles's paw reached up to his face as he rubbed his temple. "I see," he said with a sigh. "Then it seems we will have to rely on Lord Various's judgment of character. Come, I will take you to the Weavers' Guild when you are ready."

Ana nodded and rose to her feet. "I'm as ready as I'll ever be."

*   *   *

Rain was pouring down in sheets against the windows of Lord Various's office. Through the inky darkness outside, distant lights painted glittering rainbows in the droplets as they slid down the glass. A cup of tea sat on his desk atop a delicate saucer, emblazoned with the insignia of the Anvil—a gift from Carver Olen on the occasion of his wedding to Lady Sundry several years prior. Steam billowed from its surface and dissipated into the air.

Various himself sat at his desk, poring over notes, reports, addenda. A photograph of his late wife sat propped up against a pile of papers and letters.

As the elevator door slid open in the adjacent room, he rose from his seat, crossing in front of the desk.

"Kindly wait downstairs," came the voice of Cornelius from the receiving room.

"Very well" was Charles's gruff response. The door to the elevator slid shut once again.

Into the office strode Cornelius, with Ana by his side. The shapes of recently removed manacles were printed in red marks around her wrists. Her light-blue chiton hung heavily about her frame, damp from the downpour outside, and her sandals left tiny puddles in her wake.

Various pulled one of the chairs away from the desk slightly and gestured for Ana to sit. He nodded at Cornelius, who turned and walked back out to the receiving room. Crossing back to the opposite side of the desk, Various took a seat and brushed his hair away from his face, his ice-blue eyes boring deep into Ana's.

"You say that you are innocent. You accuse Ras Dashen of sneaking into the box that night to murder my wife. What proof do you have that this was the case?"

"I cannot give you any surer proof than my word," Ana began. "I don't know much about the politics of Istabar. I came here looking for someone, and I wound up in the wrong place at the wrong time. Ras Dashen gave me that Sirens' Silk to give you so that I might learn more about Amber's whereabouts. I never suspected he would use it as an opportunity to frame me for a political assassination." Ana's voice quivered as she took a step toward Various. "I have no motive, and I was as heartbroken as you were to witness Lady Sundry's murder."

Various drummed his fingers on the table. "Part of me believes you, Ana. But someone murdered my beloved Sundry, and they also escaped with the Signet of the Weavers' Guild. Captain Charles says neither you nor Ras Dashen has it. So my question to you is, where is it? One of you took it, and I want to know where it is."

Ana frowned, gazing down into her lap. Should she tell Various that she had been gifted the Signet by Lady Sundry? Should she tell him she had lost it in a hopeless errand, deep in a black morass of withered aberrations, where it would join them to rot for eternity?

Various removed a piece of parchment from the top of his pile of papers. It was stamped with the gilded symbol of the Weavers, and appeared to be an official letterhead.

"I am going to draft a recommendation tonight," Various continued. "I do not think I need to express to you further how important it is that the Signet is recovered. If you would like to give me information as to its whereabouts, I suspect the council will find it in their hearts to spare your life. If, however, you choose to remain silent on the matter, I do not know if my words will move them to mercy."

A creeping dread began to grow in the pit of Ana's stomach as the poison in Various's words washed over her. Her fists clenched into balls of anger, and her eyes flashed with a newfound menace.

"So, I ask you one final time, where is the Signet of the Weavers' Guild?"

Ana breathed in deeply, preparing her verbal assault.

"It's right here, my dear," came a voice from behind them as the elevator door slid open once again.

Out stepped Captain Charles in full armor, polearm at the ready. In his other hand, he held Malthor's sword, still in the scabbard, bright gem gleaming in its pommel. And beside him stood Lady Sundry.

She was clad in a flowing burial gown of Sirens' Silk. Its folds shimmered and shifted through innumerable hues in the dim light of the receiving room. At the shoulder, pinned to her breast, sat the tiny pin, looking for all the world as fresh as the day it was forged. Her golden hair fluttered in the still air as though caught in the shifting tides of an invisible sea. In her hand, she clutched a rolled-up piece of parchment. Ana recognized it as the Relic of Death she had so fervently scribed that night upon Malthor's Mound.

"Surprised to see me, Various?" she asked as she strode into the room, stepping lightly past a stunned Cornelius.

"Impossible" was Various's reply, as he rose to his feet behind the desk, his eyes wide with bewilderment.

"You've done me a great service, Ana. More than I ever could have asked of you. But I'm afraid I have more to ask this evening," said Sundry as she made her way into the office, Charles lagging slightly behind. "And as for my dear husband, what do you think of my new hairdo?"

"I think," said Various, reaching down under his desk, "that you should have stayed dead."

From the desk leg next to his chair, he drew his saber, casting off its sheath in one fluid movement, and leaped up over the desk. He spun head over heels in the air and landed next to Ana, facing his resurrected lover.

"My lady!" shouted Charles as he tossed Malthor's sword through the air. Reaching out, Cornelius attempted an intercept but succeeded only in knocking it out of the air. Seizing the opportunity of Sundry's momentary distraction, Various lunged forward, the saber whistling through the air. Ana thrust out her leg instinctively, catching Various's back foot and sending him tumbling off course toward the side of the room. Her eyes fell on the sword, now lying on the ground between herself and Cornelius.

Meanwhile, Cornelius had turned on Charles and charged, colliding with the captain and sending both of them crashing into the elevator. Charles's polearm caught on the doorframe and clattered back into the receiving room. Scrabbling to his feet, Cornelius mashed the elevator's lobby button and stepped back. Charles rose to his feet slowly, the bulky armor dragging him back down as he slipped on the rain-slick floor of the lift. The door to the elevator slid shut and began its descent back down to the ground floor, Charles with it.

Recovering his balance, Various rushed forward, his blade flickering through the air. It narrowly missed Sundry's throat as she bent backward and flipped deftly into the receiving room. She crouched down to grab Charles's discarded polearm and caught Cornelius on the upswing, knocking him back onto the couches. Sundry then started toward Various but was suddenly on the floor as Cornelius caught her leg from behind. The two hit the ground and began to grapple over the polearm, struggling back and forth as its blade skittered across the wooden floor.

Approaching from above, Various swung out with his saber, narrowly missing Sundry's chest as she and Cornelius wrestled on the floor. As he withdrew the saber for a second attempt, he felt a sharp, searing pain in his calf. Spinning about, he came face-to-face with Ana, who was wielding Malthor's sword, its tip streaked with blood.

"You wretch!" He lashed out, his blade clattering against hers with a deafening crack. Lifting her sword up, she buckled under the force of the blow and slid to the side. He followed her around, brandishing the saber and swinging wildly at her face. She backed up and fell backward onto the top of his desk, sending papers and other paraphernalia flying across the room as she landed. In an instant, he was upon her again, raising his sword high above his head and bringing it down in a deadly coup de grâce.

Swinging her sword up, Ana caught the saber's edge in the groove of her blade. She pushed forward and redirected the sword into the desk, where it glanced off to the side. Shoving her legs up, she pushed into Various's chest and lifted him up, over her head, and straight into the panoramic window behind them.

As he collided with the surface, it shattered into countless razor-sharp shards as he flew out and onto the balcony outside.

Dropping off the desk, Ana continued out into the blinding rain and surging wind. Rising from the deck, covered in blood and fringed with the tatters of his black overcoat, Various seethed with hatred.

"I will not be bested by you, outsider," he hissed through gritted teeth.

Once again he was upon her, swinging wildly through the rain, each blow caught and countered by Ana as they danced across the shards of shattered glass. Again and again he swung, and the ferocity of his attack began to beat a perilous weight into her arms. The sword grew heavier and heavier, and her grip on it began to slip as water and blood weaved their way down between her fingers.

Suddenly her foot slid forward on a slick sliver of glass, and she tumbled back, landing on the edge of the balcony as her hair dangled over the streets of Istabar many stories below. The sword clattered out of her hand, and Various stood over her, raising his sword once again for the final strike. Blinded now by the driving rain, Ana brought her hand up over her eyes and braced for the rending saber.

A sickly squelching sound filled her ears as she felt a sudden warmth flooding across her abdomen. As she wiped the rainwater from her eyes and looked up, she saw Various, still standing over her, as his saber hit the ground with a loud clang. The tip of a polearm was protruding straight out of his midsection, blood pouring from the wound, down across the blade, and pooling on her stomach. Various lurched forward and fell past her, toppling off the roof and tumbling through the air, down toward the darkened streets far below.

Sundry bent down and grasped Ana's forearm, pulling her gently up to her feet and ushering her back into the office. Ana was shaking violently, though whether from the chill of the rain or the slowly fading adrenaline, she couldn't say.

In the receiving room, Cornelius shuffled along, bound and gagged, as Charles pushed him forward into the elevator.

"That was quite a performance," he said, smiling. "Where did you learn to fight like that?"

Ana could offer no reply, still swimming in the shock of her victory.

"I'm going to take this fellow off to visit the prison for a while," he continued. "Probably quite a while, if I had to guess." Charles shoved Cornelius, cowed and quaking, into the elevator, and the two of them disappeared down the shaft.

As Ana and Sundry were waiting for the lift to return, Sundry took Ana by the hand and led her to one of the couches lining the side of the receiving room.

"I can't thank you enough, you know," whispered Sundry. "I knew Various was going to try something, but I had no idea he could be so brazen as to do it in public … and so cowardly as to hire someone else to do it for him."

Ana put her head on Sundry's shoulder, her shivering beginning to soften.

"Why don't you come back to my residence this evening? We'll get you cleaned up—and I suspect you'll find our beds quite a bit more comfortable than a prison cot."

Ana nodded, and as the elevator once again returned to the top floor, the two women stood and left the ruined office behind them.

19

Ana fumbled with her keys as she attempted to unlock the door to her apartment. They slipped out of her hand and landed with a jingling thud on the carpeted hallway floor. She sighed and shifted her arms around as she carefully lowered her grocery bags to the ground. After scooping up the keys, she brought them once again to the lock just as the knob turned and the door swung open, revealing Amber's face. Her smile was warm, but the bags under her eyes betrayed a deep exhaustion—even getting up from the couch to open the door was almost too much to ask these days, and Ana regretted her clumsiness.

"Aw, what's wrong?" asked Amber, sensing her partner's dismay.

"I'm fine, just clumsy—dropped the keys on the ground, that's all."

Amber reached out to take one of the grocery bags, but Ana refused to give them up. She waddled her way into the kitchen and deposited the load on the table, smoothing out her shirt as she returned the keys to a peg on the wall. As she returned to the table, Amber was busy pulling items out of bags and sorting them into the pantry.

"It's okay, really, I've got it," said Ana as she shooed Amber away from the table.

"Oh, nonsense," came Amber's reply as she gamely continued to bustle about the kitchen, placing spices on the spice rack and milk in the refrigerator. Rummaging around toward the bottom of one of the bags, she pulled out a cardboard box with a vacuum-formed plastic display piece in the front. Through the transparent cover, she could see a set of electric hair clippers, with a variety of settings ranging from upward of an inch down to essentially nothing.

"Ooh, is this for me?"

Ana turned, unsure of how to broach the subject of Amber's increasingly sparse coiffure.

"I just thought …" she began.

"You just thought that you'd like to stop pulling all my hair out of the drain, hmm?" said Amber with a playful nudge. "Sounds like fun; I'm excited to look like the girl from *Mad Max*."

"I know you could rock whatever haircut you wanted, but I figured if you really wanted to commit to the whole 'cancer patient' thing, you should start to look the part."

"I'm down," said Amber, tearing the cardboard apart and popping open the plastic casing. "Why don't you pour us some wine while I get set up in the bathroom?"

She disappeared around the corner with the clippers, leaving Ana alone in the kitchen.

Ana walked back over to the table slowly, collecting the discarded packaging and depositing it in a paper bag on the counter that doubled as the recycling bin. On top of the fridge stood several bottles of wine, most of them previously opened. She pulled the cork out of the top of one of the bottles and sniffed, recoiling slightly at the sharp scent of vinegar. Continuing on down the line, she inspected each bottle until she came upon a Malbec that still seemed to have some life left in it.

She took it down and poured two glasses, carrying them around the corner and down the hall to the bathroom. Amber had set up a desk chair in front of the mirror, and a portable hand vacuum sat on top of the closed toilet lid. Walking into the bathroom behind Ana, Amber reentered the space and draped a towel over the back of the office chair. She was wearing what appeared to be a Superman cape, backward across her front, as a makeshift barber's smock.

"Okay, I'm ready," she said, taking a seat in the chair. She plugged in the clippers and handed them to Ana, who had stepped up behind her. The two women locked eyes in the mirror, and Ana could at once see the tears beginning to well up in Amber's eyes.

"Are you sure you want to do this?" asked Ana, feeling tears of her own start to choke her voice.

Amber's smile quivered for a moment, but she nodded sharply. "*Fury Road*, here we come."

Ana clicked on the clippers. The sharp buzzing sound drilled into their ears, its deep drone heralding the point of no return. Slowly she approached Amber's messy blond locks, raising the implement as one would heft a butcher's cleaver.

Just as the clippers reached their target, Amber cried, "Wait!"

Ana withdrew, clicking off the clippers and gazing at her partner in the mirror.

"Before you take it all off … give me a Mohawk first."

*   *   *

Lady Sundry's residence was an immaculate manse on one of the upper tiers of the city, fairly close to the Weavers' Guild itself. Inside, its decor was not unlike the now-ruined office of Lord Various—of course, he must have lived here too. Beautiful tapestries adorned every wall, depicting the great history of Istabar, from its founding in the age of antiquity right through to the present day.

The sheets upon the bed in the guesthouse were some of the most incredible pieces of cloth Ana had ever encountered—it felt as though she were being wrapped in a warm river, so smooth and light were their construction. Their soothing embrace seemed to put a great deal of distance between her and the traumatic events of the evening prior, though she knew that the sting of Lord Various's betrayal would stay with her for many days to come.

Ana had crossed over a small bridge flanked with shimmering sheets of water and entered the residence proper. To her surprise, Sundry was busy in the expansive kitchen, preparing breakfast for herself and her guest.

"Ah, good morning," she said with a cheerful lilt. "I trust the room was sufficient?"

"Oh, more than sufficient—I can't thank you enough for allowing me to sleep here last night."

"Please, my dear, you brought me back from the brink of eternity. You saved my life, and as such, I owe you a debt I can never repay. You are welcome here for as long as you remain in our city, and for every visit thereafter."

She smiled warmly and placed a bowl heaping with scrambled eggs onto the table.

"I'm just finishing up with the waffles. Olen gifted me a waffle iron a few birthdays ago, and to be honest, I've never used it, so I've burnt the first few batches—but I'm getting the hang of it!"

Ana walked up along the expansive table and pulled out a chair, taking a seat near the action as Sundry flipped some rather crispy waffles out of a large iron and onto a plate.

"I'm awfully glad you met up with Doro," Sundry continued. "He's about the only person on the Isle of Hope who knows the deeper secrets … intervening with the forces of life—and death."

Carrying the waffles over, she took a seat next to Ana and began to pile food onto their plates, first Ana's, and then her own.

"You know, I found out only a few days before we met that Various was up to something. To his credit, he was a shrewd man, as mischievous in the council chamber as he was in the sack." She waggled an eyebrow at Ana, who was already forkfuls deep into the feast. "But all good things must come to an end, and I think he grew to resent me after a time."

Ana looked up from her plate to cast an inquisitive eye at Sundry, who was slathering her waffles with maple syrup.

"I knew he was envious of my position on the council. And I suppose for good reason. I am a daughter of the Bank of Drasz, and my election to the council on behalf of the Weavers was less than devoid of privilege. But I never imagined he would stoop so low, until one of my little birdies uncovered the missive he had sent to Ras Dashen."

"So you knew that Ras Dashen was out to get you?"

"Indeed. That is why I gave you the Signet. I had my people working on a solution for Ras Dashen, but I needed an insurance policy in case my timeline didn't work out. And indeed, it did not. But beyond the safekeeping of the Signet with a neutral party, I never intended for you to be involved in the political machinations of Istabar, and for that I am deeply sorry."

Ana shook her head in deference, her mouth stuffed with food.

"In any case, the past is now behind us. The council is now aware of Lord Various's treachery. Charles has informed them of last night's events, and all charges against you have been dropped."

Ana was speechless. For the first time since that night at the opera, she felt she could breathe again, free from the overwhelming dread of persecution.

"Ras Dashen's life, however, is about to get significantly more challenging," said Sundry with a grin.

Ana sat for a moment staring down at her plate. Looking back up at Sundry, she frowned. "Can I ask you something?"

"Of course, dear. Anything." A look of concern flashed across Sundry's face.

"When you came back … at Malthor's Mound … did you see Doro?"

Sundry sat back in her chair, gazing toward the ceiling in contemplation.

"My memory is foggy, I'm afraid. I remember the tree … and the Signet … and your letter." She gestured to the parchment, rolled up and sitting on the counter nearby. "I remember walking in circles for many hours. I remember eyes in the darkness. But I do not remember Doro."

Ana sighed. "I hope he's okay."

"Oh, of course he's okay." Sundry reached over to place a hand on Ana's shoulder. "He's the Shepherd of Hope."

"That night, in the swamp, Doro told me something. He said he'd been speaking to Olen. And Olen said he might have something that would help me find Amber. I think he called it a Periapt of Pursuit."

Sundry raised an eyebrow. "Well, I don't know what that is, but if anyone has a bead on some sort of person-finding gadget, it's probably Olen."

Ana sighed. "I suppose it's pretty difficult to get an audience with members of the council."

"Generally, yes. But not for you. Why don't you get suited up, and we'll head over to the Anvil? I'm sure he won't mind if we drop in."

Ana's eyes lit up. She practically jumped from her chair, eager to pursue the first proper lead she'd had since her arrival at the Midnight Beach. Sundry smiled, clearing the dishes and placing them in the sink.

In a moment, the two were out the door.

*   *   *

The Anvil stood, true to its name, as a giant anvil towering over the streets of the crafting district in Istabar. It was one of the few buildings not fashioned from white stone; rather, it seemed almost cast iron in appearance. At its foot, a great archway led inside, and past that, the air was hot with the great gust of bellows, stoking furnaces and breathing life into the monumental structure.

Down into the depths of the structure they wandered, first through two enormous iron doors, then down a stone staircase, switching back and forth as the room around them opened up to reveal a huge cauldron lined with tiny workshops. In them, stout little men and women hammered away at various creations—weapons, tools, parts, fixtures—building the components that supported the infrastructure of the city.

At the base of the cauldron seethed a pool of what looked to be molten rock or metal, and just above it, a stone walkway. The stairwell twisted down and out onto the walkway.

"Watch your step," said Sundry as they made their way across.

In the middle of the walkway was a large anvil, the mirror of the one they now stood inside, and Ana suspected this was its prototype. Continuing on past the monument, the walkway opened into a small hall, circular in shape. In the center of the room was a large iron desk, at which sat Carver Olen, who was tinkering with some small mechanical component.

"Carver," Sundry called out. Olen looked up from his contraption, his eye rendered huge through a magnifying glass fixed to an articulated arm mounted on his tabletop.

"Well, as I live and breathe, Lady Sundry. I heard the tale from Captain Charles, and even so, I can scarcely believe it." He rose from the desk and crossed around it, walking toward her with arms stretched open in welcome. "To return from the Gyrewood … it's not been done for a thousand years at least. But if anyone could do it, sure it's ye."

The two embraced, Olen's head barely reaching her stomach. Sundry laughed and put a hand on his shoulder. "Well, it wouldn't have happened at all if not for Ana here."

"Aye, it seems we owe ye a great debt," said Olen with a nod. He leaned in toward Ana. "And for the record, I voted for the mistrial," he said with a sly wink.

"So, what brings the two of ye down to my humble forge? Come to chuck that rat bastard Various's corpse into the furnace?"

"In fact, we've come for some advice," said Sundry, gesturing back to Ana.

"While Doro and I were walking in the Gyrewood, he mentioned that he met with you last week. He said you might have something that could help me find my friend."

"Ah yes," said Olen, "the Periapt of Pursuit. I do recall this chat."

Walking back to the rear of his office, Olen began to look up and down the immense bookcases lining the walls. The shelves were connected to one another via a sort of brass railing that ran around the circumference of the room. Pulling a very tall ladder around on this track, he slid it into place and clambered up, sifting around in the stacks until at last he found what he was looking for. He removed a musty old tome from one of the shelves and descended the ladder, carrying it back over to Ana and Sundry. He hefted it onto the top of the desk in an explosion of dust and began to carefully flip through its ancient pages.

"Yes, here we are," Olen said at last. "The Periapt of Pursuit—a tool for finding anyone, anywhere. Once attuned to an individual, the periapt will guide the wielder to the whereabouts of said individual, no matter their location."

"That's incredible," said Ana. "And you have one of these?"

"Not exactly, no," said Olen with a frown. "But we *can* make one, with the right materials."

"So what do we need?" asked Sundry.

"Well, there aren't too many ingredients, thankfully. But some might be a bit challenging to acquire. We'll need a bag of sand, but not just any sand—it has to be the Sands of Time. That shouldn't be too difficult though—the Midnight Beach is covered with it. We'll also need an ingot of pure orichalcum—I think the mystics up on Mount Rhos might be able to help us out there. And lastly, a Relic of Life for the person ye want to find."

"Well, that doesn't sound too bad," said Sundry, looking over the cryptic symbols written across the book's weathered pages.

"Here's the thing though: once we've got all this stuff, we can't just slap it together anywhere. We're gonna need to fashion the lens and forge the setting in a specific place. Specifically the Forge of Nightmares. On the Isle of Fear."

"That sounds bad," said Sundry.

Ana frowned. "And I don't really have a relic of Amber's life."

"Well, what about the dagger? We know she bought it for some reason or other—it belonged to her, however briefly," said Sundry.

"That might work, yeah," said Olen, stroking his prodigious beard.

"How hard is it to get to the Forge of Nightmares?" asked Ana as she pored over the ancient diagrams and illustrations in the book.

"It's not exactly a walk in the park. But not impossible. And seein' as how ye went out of yer way to resurrect our dear Lady Sundry here, 'twould be the least I could do to help ye find yer missing lady."

Rolling up the sleeves of his smock, Olen closed the book and slid it off to the side of the desk, rolling out a map in its place.

"Right, then, let's get to it!"

20

It took Sundry and Ana the rest of the morning and well into midafternoon to make the trek back down out of the hills and down again into the dunes just east of the Midnight Beach. The coast was not a place many people frequented, and that fact, combined with the difficult terrain, meant that there was no more expeditious transit option than one's own two feet.

On the way, their conversation was lively—Sundry told Ana of her history with Various, of the slowly creeping realization of his betrayal, of her anguish at his treachery, held silently for fear of a preemptive attack, and of her surprise at his brazen assassination attempt in the opera that night.

Ana told Sundry about her arrival on the Isle of Hope and her first encounter with Doro. She spoke about running into Ras Dashen at the crossroads, her first meeting with Various, the night at the opera, her subsequent incarceration and escape, spiders in the woods, and the horrors of Malthor's Mound.

"So Doro broke open the mound, and you fell in?" asked Sundry.

"Yeah—and the ceiling caved in behind me."

"My goodness. How did you manage to get out?"

"Well, there was a riddle written inside the tomb, and when I figured out the answer, a passageway opened up into some catacombs below. I followed the tunnels for what seemed like ages. There were recesses in the walls filled with bones and cobwebs, and tons of little intersections and corridors. It was a maze down there.

"There were also these inscriptions in the walls, and when I spoke out loud, they spelled messages back to me. Whatever was down there seemed to know about Amber. I tried to get it to tell me where she was, but I couldn't get a straight answer. It did help me get out of the catacombs though ... but not before I was attacked by a bunch of giant spiders."

"Ugh, that's awful," said Sundry.

"Thankfully, at that point, I was pretty close to an exit. I dodged one of the big ones, and it knocked a huge stone door open. That was the first time I'd seen sunlight since we'd entered the swamp. The door was built into a little hill—I walked out of it and found myself in a cemetery on the edge of the Gyrewood. I could see some small buildings in the distance, so I headed for the town—I didn't know what else to do."

"And that's how you ended up in Peju."

Ana nodded. "By the time I got there, it was getting dark, so I hopped a fence on the outskirts of the village and wandered through the streets until I got to the pier. I saw some of Captain Charles's guards walking the streets, and I figured they were looking for me, so I snuck into an empty shop through an open window and hid there for a couple of hours. I was planning on scrounging some food and heading back to the woods for the night—that's when I saw Ras Dashen cowering behind a building down the street."

"You figured he was your ticket back to Istabar if you could get a confession out of him?"

"I tried, but I think he really was in the dark about who'd hired him. Various played his cards close to the chest."

"Yes, he always was an astucious sort of fellow," said Sundry as she gazed off toward the winding road ahead.

For a while, the two women continued in silence, until eventually Sundry spoke up again. "Tell me about Amber."

Ana smiled. "She's really cute. Curly blond hair. Wears glasses that are a little bit too big for her face. I don't think there's anything in the world she likes more than inflicting terrible puns on people—"

"I meant, tell me about what happened. How she ended up here."

Ana's pace slowed. The wind picked up for a moment, sending little whirling clouds of sand dancing through the valleys between the dunes.

"You must love her very much," said Sundry. "To come all the way out here to look for her."

"I didn't know what else to do," said Ana. "I know she'd come looking for me."

As they crested the final dune atop the cliffs, a deep steel-blue ocean stretched out before them under an infinite slate-grey sky. Deep in her chest, Ana felt a sudden pang of longing. Breaking into a jog, she skirted the edge of the cliffs and followed the path down along the rocks, cutting back and forth through the stones until she came into a small open area. A sea cave sat here, the wind whistling gently through its opening as the deep rumble of subterranean waves churned far below.

"Doro!" she cried, running into the mouth of the cave. As she wound down through the entrance, the walls glittered with soft light from the lamps suspended above. "Doro?" As she reached the bottom of the entryway and walked into the larger cavern below, her calls were met with silence.

"Ana?" came Sundry's voice from high above as she poked her head into the cave. "Are you okay? Is he in there?"

"He's not," she called back as she turned to make her way back out of the cave. After walking up and out past Sundry, into the cool ocean air once again, she braced herself against a low wall, then slid down to the ground, protected there from the urgent offshore breeze.

"I just figured he'd either come here or go to Istabar after he got out of the swamp—*if* he got out of the swamp."

Sundry knelt down and put her hand on Ana's shoulder. "Not to worry. Doro can take care of himself. And who knows? We might run into him on the way back to the city," she said, standing up straight once again. "But we've got a job to do right now, and if we want to be back by dark, we've got to do it posthaste."

Ana gazed down at the wind-polished rock for a moment, then lifted herself up and nodded.

Continuing down the cliff face, the two women wound back and forth along the path until it slowly dissolved into sand. Putting a hand on her sword to steady it against the blustery sea spray, Ana marched forward across the beach, sidestepping clumps of kelp and the brittle remains of lost sand dollars.

At last she reached the border with the sea as the tide swelled up to gently kiss her ankles. Here, even in the relative brightness of daylight, she could sense the ethereal silvery glow of the sand. It had a sort of otherworldly quality to it, enriched by the whispers of distant waves.

Sundry strode up behind her and handed her a simple jar. Bending down, Ana scooped handful upon handful of bright sand and sea-foam into the container. When it was full to the brim, she clamped on its metal lid and handed it back to Sundry for safekeeping.

"Well, mission accomplished," said Ana, brushing her hands together in a cloud of shimmering sand.

"Let's get back to the city," said Sundry. "The road gets a lot less safe after dark."

*　　*　　*

Many miles east of the Midnight Beach, and many miles south of Istabar, rose the imposing summit of Mount Rhos. As the meeting point between two ranges, the top of the mountain dwarfed its neighboring peaks and stood alone as the highest point on the Isle of Hope. Row upon row of spruce, pine, and fir slowly gave way to bare stone as Olen continued his ascent beyond the tree line. The air was frigid, and day-old snowfall hid in the shadows of trees and rocks as he ambled up the mountainside.

Atop this towering peak sat the Shrine of the Bird of Passage—a monument built in ages past, hewn into the very stone of the mountain, then expanded with lumber from its slopes. To ascend to the shrine was no easy task, but once there, the view it commanded was second to none. As the lower forests shrank into mossy specks beyond the timberline, the precipitous pathway became a flight of stone stairs. Olen continued to make his way up the mountain, one step at a time.

He was above the clouds now, and the air seemed whisper-thin, but still he climbed, the shrine now barely visible in the distance. Step after step, he pressed on, until at last, after eleven thousand one hundred and eleven stone steps, he reached the top of the mountain. The land was barren here, almost lunar in appearance, save for a handful of small, hardy trees rooted in rough-hewn stone planters. They were no doubt meticulously maintained by the monks who tended to the shrine.

Bustling about in bright yellow robes were large yet nimble-looking goat-people, tending to the sparse gardens, porting well water, and otherwise busying themselves around the summit. The biting wind and fierce cold did not seem to concern the methodical ungulates, though Olen could not say the same for himself. His panting and wheezing drew the attention of one of the monks, who came rushing over to assist.

"Friend, are you alright? Has the stairway gotten the best of you, perhaps?" He laughed. "Here, come inside. We have tea and a warm fire waiting."

The woolly creature guided Olen to the main structure, a large wooden edifice, inside which the old stone building could still be seen. The great doors swung open as if they were made of air, so precise was the workmanship on the hinges. Following into the great hall, Olen could smell the deep, fresh scent of spices wafting in from the communal kitchen. They worked their way through and into a waiting area just outside the old central building.

Sitting down at a table, Olen could see there were a handful of other pilgrims who had chosen to make the trek that day, each wrapped in a warm blanket, still recovering from their ordeal. In a moment, the cloven-hoofed monk had returned with a small bowl of hot lentil soup and a cup of what smelled like barley tea.

"Here, friend, drink deep. And spend some time in the hall here while you acclimate to the altitude."

"Thank ye kindly, good monk," said Olen, still quite out of breath from the last few thousand steps.

As the monk turned back to resume his duties outside, Olen spoke out. "Wait!"

Turning around again, the monk smiled attentively.

"It's been many years since last I've made the trip up to the Shrine of the Bird of Passage. Tell me, does Thokcha still preside over the inner sanctum?"

"She does indeed," said the monk, bowing deeply. "If you like, I would be happy to inform her of your arrival."

"I'd like that very much, thank ye."

"Very well—and what name should I give her, friend?"

"Ah, apologies—it's Carver Olen, on behalf of the Ruling Council of Istabar."

At this, the goat's ears flared back, and he once again bowed deeply. "I did not realize, sir. It is an honor. I will fetch Thokcha at once."

As the monk disappeared around the corner of the small interior shrine, Olen sat and admired the beautiful fabrics, small flags, and gentle peace that pervaded the atmosphere inside the wooden building.

Several minutes later, another goat in a yellow robe, this one with a wreath of wild mountain flowers arrayed about her head, walked into the room.

"Olen, my old friend, how are you?"

"Not too much worse for wear, though I still say ye could stand to have an elevator installed." Olen rose from his chair to be enveloped in a broad embrace.

"It's been so long!" Thokcha's voice was tipped with a gentle lilt. She slid onto a small bench opposite the haggard-looking councillor. "What brings you to our quiet mountain home?"

"Well, to be honest with ye, I've a favor to ask."

"You and the Anvil have ever been a friend to my people," she said warmly. "If it is in my power, you have but to ask."

"You remember the figurines we sent up here for the Wintertide Festival ten or so years back?"

"Of course. They're beautiful. I have them in the interior shrine, just above the prayer wheel you made for us last year."

"Well, here's the thing. There's a lass who's lost a dear friend of hers, and we're trying to find her. I need a bar of orichalcum to whip her up a trinket what'll help her track this lady down, and we're fresh out down at the foundry. There's only so much of that stuff on the Isle of Hope, and we haven't gotten a shipment of outside ore in years. So I'm askin' ye, let me borrow the figurines back. I'll happily make ye something else in return."

"Oh, my dear Olen, we don't deal in trades on this mountain. Gifts are gifts, freely given. And this is a gift I happily give to you."

Thokcha rose from her seat at the table and beckoned Olen onward. The two walked up to the small interior shrine, and she held out her hand, inviting him inside.

Within the humble exterior was a treasure trove beyond imagination. Items and trinkets so valuable as to be priceless sat here, utterly unguarded save for a universal understanding that these items were beyond the ken of mortals. As Olen glanced up and down the room, it shimmered with gold, jewels, and ornate statues. Prayer wheels and small implements of faith spun quietly of their own accord, pulsing with a devotion at once foreign to Olen and yet deeply familiar. And there, next to a large wheel inscribed with strange, shifting symbols, was a set of four small statues in the shape of Thokcha's people.

"They are yours," said Thokcha. "Take them with my blessing. May they serve you well on your noble quest."

21

As the evening light began to once again paint the walls of Istabar with a deep, rosy orange, Ana and Sundry were on their way back through the main gate. The guards on either side of the street saluted them with respect, while onlookers pressed in on all sides to witness the miracle of Lady Sundry's return to the land of the living. The pair wound their way through the labyrinthine streets and alleyways to the crafting district, then up into the Anvil's namesake headquarters and down into its fiery depths. Across the great stone span they went, and into Carver Olen's office.

There, on Olen's desk, lay the menacing dagger that had taken Sundry's life—evidently, he'd brought it over from the Tower of Drasz prior to departing for Mount Rhos. As Sundry's eyes fell upon its barbed blade, she shivered.

"Are you alright?" asked Ana, walking over to put her hand on Sundry's shoulder.

"That thing," said Sundry, "was the last thing I remember before I died. That awful thing plunging into my chest, piercing my lungs. I tried to scream, but the air just gushed out of the wound, and my voice went with it."

"I'm sorry. Here, let's put it in a drawer, or—"

"No, it's fine," Sundry reassured her. "Really. It's just an inert hunk of metal. It's not going to end any more lives, and if we're lucky, it might just save one."

Reaching into her satchel, Sundry produced the jar containing the Sands of Time, gathered fresh that afternoon from the Midnight Beach. She placed it on the desk next to the dagger and turned back to Ana.

"Well, we're two-thirds of the way there. If Olen comes through with the orichalcum, we're in business."

"And then we have to take all of this stuff to the Forge of Nightmares?" asked Ana.

"So it would seem."

"Doesn't sound like a very inviting place."

"It's not," said Sundry. "Well, I've never been there, but if it's anything like the rest of the Isle of Fear, it's no summer holiday."

"What's the Isle of Fear like?"

Sundry thought for a moment, rapping her fingers lightly on the desk behind her.

"We've probably got some time until Olen comes back down off that mountain. Come with me, and I'll show you."

*　　*　　*

Ana and Sundry stood before a large but otherwise fairly unremarkable building just a few doors down from the entrance to the Tower of Drasz. It had some small columns out front—a sign over the door read "Archive."

"A rare interguild collaboration," said Sundry. "The archive was one of the first structures erected in Istabar after the tower. And it remains to this day a partnership between the scribes and record-keepers of each guild. All of Istabar's history is chronicled somewhere within these walls, though certainly not all of it is particularly worth reading.

"What we're here for, though, has little to do with Istabar. The archive also keeps a great deal of information on file about the rest of the isles, including the Isle of Fear."

Sundry gestured toward the door, and Ana took the lead and entered the building.

At the front desk sat what appeared to be a corgi in some sort of bellhop outfit, complete with tiny fez. The dog was fast asleep. Walking past the diminutive clerk, they came to a large winding staircase that spiraled up through the ceiling. They followed it several stories up, until it opened out into an ornate library built around a large atrium space. Ana could at once smell the rich, dusty aroma of wood pulp and binding that permeated the air.

The walls were lined with multiple separate levels of stacks, packed to the brim with books, maps, and all manner of other publications. A variety of patrons milled about in silence, hunting through the vast collection for a specific scrap of knowledge.

Sundry walked over to the wall and gestured for Ana to follow. Around the back of a stack of books was a tiny set of stairs that led up to the second and third levels of the shelf area. As they climbed up the narrow steps in single file, Sundry whispered to Ana in a hushed tone that betrayed her reverence for the antiquated athenaeum.

"Olen's spent more time on the Isle of Fear than anyone else I know. In his younger days, he was quite the treasure hunter. He came here to learn about the island. Sometimes, on the way home after a late-night session in the council chamber, I would stop by this library just to get lost in the books and … I don't know … unwind, I suppose. Often I'd find him here, poring over some ancient piece of nearly forgotten knowledge."

Cresting the final step, the two women emerged on the second level of the library, overlooking the open space below. Around the corner was a section marked "Reference." Plunging into the shelves, Sundry weeded through the stacks, zeroing in on a subsection labeled "Beyond Hope."

"One night, while he was telling me of one of his travels to the isle, he showed me a book. I couldn't make out whatever lost tongue it was penned in, but the hand-drawn illustrations stand out vividly in my mind."

Picking through the individual tomes, she at last pulled out a prodigious leather-bound volume. On its cover was a title, inscribed in gilded runes that Ana could not decipher.

"*A Bestiary of the Isle of Fear*," said Sundry as she hefted it off the shelf and onto a nearby table for further inspection. "Or at any rate, I think that's what he called it."

"Why *is* it called that?" asked Ana.

"The Isle of Fear is so named because it is a place where the natural spirits and creatures of the land have gone mad. Long ago, the Servants of Disaster tried to pull a great calamity into this world. The aperture through which this horror nearly made landfall was deep within the island. Though the Servants ultimately did not succeed, the land has been tainted with corruption ever since. No peaceful life remains. It is simply a battle-scarred hellscape upon which crazed elementals wage war upon one another for all eternity."

As Ana flipped through the pages, her attention was drawn to an illustrated image of what appeared to be a hulking lump of moss, stone, and human bones. It was easily several stories high—it towered above the treetops drawn below. In general construction, it seemed similar to Cromag, the brave archer who had given his life to defend Ana and Doro in the Gyrewood—though this creature was much larger. In addition, there was something off about the construct's demeanor. A curious black flame seemed to float about the area where its head should have been. Ana wondered if this was a literal observation or perhaps some poetic license on behalf of the illustrator.

"Olen called those things 'gravewalkers,'" said Sundry. "They rise up out of ancient burial mounds and stalk around the island, looking to add to their collection of corpses. Generally, they do not wait for you to die first."

Turning the page over, there was another illustration. A forest was alight with flames in the background. In the foreground, several small, impish-looking balls of fire with arms and legs cavorted around a smoking tree. They, too, were fringed with some haunting oily tendrils of black flame.

"These are emberlings. They seek to cover the island in fire and reduce its surface to ash. Consequently, much of the island is burning at any given moment."

Continuing to flip through the book, Ana uncovered page after page of elemental aberrations, each more twisted and tortured than the last.

"And you said the Servants of Disaster did all this? Are they some sort of cult or something?"

"They were," said Sundry, closing the book and hefting it back onto the shelf from whence it had come. "The Servants tried to force some horrible monster into our world that wasn't supposed to be here. The then residents of the place that would come to be known as the Isle of Fear managed to prevent this from happening, but they lost their home in the process. No one really knows what happened to them after that. This all happened a long, long time ago—no such cult still remains.

"But there is a structure near the center of the island. It's an ancient crucible, a place for manufacturing weapons and armor. It is now called the Forge of Nightmares, and there is a deep magic about this place that is apparently necessary for the construction of the amulet we need to find Amber."

"So how do I get there?" asked Ana.

"Well, for starters, we'll need to catch a flight."

*   *   *

The following morning, Ana, Sundry, and Olen were all aboard the train to Peju. As the miles clipped by, Ana glanced around at her traveling companions. Sundry looked ready for battle. She had raided the small armory in her mansion and come away with an elegant set of leather armor and an elaborate longbow. Olen had been kind enough to supply her with a number of arrows from the Anvil's reserve.

The dwarf himself looked somewhat worse for wear and was asleep across several seats. He had returned from the mountain quite late the evening prior, but he had returned victorious, and in a large satchel, he carried the dagger, the jar of sand, and four small statuettes of shimmering orichalcum. He had also taken the time to equip himself with some shining plate mail and an imposing one-handed maul, the end of which was shaped like a blacksmith's hammer. At his side rested a shield bearing the gleaming sigil of the Anvil.

For Ana's part, she had gratefully accepted the addition of some brilliant chain mail. For all its tangible strength, it felt almost weightless under her chiton. Malthor's sword hung gracefully from her belt as she pondered its pommel's mysterious glow.

As the click-clack of the train across the tracks slowed to a snail's pace, Ana looked out the window to see the familiar shingled roofs and tiered buildings of Peju rising in the distance. She felt a pang of unease, though in her mind she knew that this time she arrived as a champion, not a fugitive. The brakes squealed as they ground the carriage to a halt, and the doors swung open to reveal helmeted fish-people ushering passengers out of the train and into the station.

Ana and her companions disembarked and made their way out of the building and down to the pier at the end of the street. Stopping off at the harbormaster's office, Sundry procured three tickets for the Isle of Fear.

"You mean there's blimp service to the Isle of Fear?" asked Ana, arching an eyebrow. "I thought it was abandoned and full of monsters."

"Well, it basically is abandoned and full of monsters," said Olen, "but some crazy folks like to head out there on occasion to try and pick up rare materials and suchlike. So the port maintains a flight, once a day, there and back."

"Indeed," said Sundry, stepping away from the window with tickets in hand. "There is a small settlement on the southeastern coast—little more than a trading post, really, but it's where we'll have to stay while we wait for tomorrow's flight back to Peju … assuming we make it back from the Forge of Nightmares in one piece."

"Three pieces," said Olen. "If we come back as one piece, we've messed something up."

"You two really don't have to do this. Amber's my girlfriend, and it's my responsibility to find her, not yours."

"You saved my life," said Sundry. "And given where we're headed, chances are good I'll soon have the opportunity to return the favor." She hefted her bow up onto her shoulder and started down the pier to the tower to which was moored the curious floating jellyfish.

"You really don't have to do this, Olen. You've already helped so much in finding the orichalcum," said Ana.

"I pretty much do, lass—unless ye've learned to smelt magical metals since yesterday." Olen laughed. "Besides, who knows what other great stuff we'll discover at the forge? It's finders keepers out there on the Isle of Fear, after all. I love a good adventure!" Olen took off down the pier after Sundry, leaving Ana alone to ponder the remarkable fortitude of her newfound friends.

I hope our paths cross again someday, she thought as the gentle wooden visage of Doro crossed her mind.

After a moment, she joined them in climbing up the winding stairs to the boarding platform of the blimp. Suspended below the hulking jellyfish was a wooden gondola, and passengers were filtering in one by one. A fish-person punched the tickets as they crossed the gangway onto the blimp.

"Seems like an awful lot of people heading to the Isle of Fear," said Ana.

"I bet we're the only ones headed there today," Olen replied. "This ship'll carry on towards the Isle of Truth after it drops us off."

The three shuffled forward. Ana held out her ticket to be punched, and then boarded the craft, feeling it rock back and forth gently as it swayed and bobbed in the wind.

"What's on the Isle of Truth?" asked Ana as Olen stepped in behind her.

"Only what ye bring with ye," said Olen.

"The Isle of Truth is different for everyone who goes there," said Sundry from a bench seat near the front of the gondola. She patted the seat next to her, inviting her companions to join her as the last few passengers filtered aboard. "Everyone experiences it in a different way. So it's hard to say what it's like in general, but for most people, it's a great place to be."

As Ana was pondering how such a strange place could exist, the gondola lurched as the man-of-war's tendrils gave up their hold on the mooring tower. Floating off into the air, Ana looked back at the little village of Peju, fading into the fog below. She thought of her tiny apartment and wondered if she and Amber would ever enjoy another quiet moment cramped within its walls.

22

Several hours after their departure from Peju, the acrid scent of burning wood began to fill the gondola. At once Ana was on her feet, scouting around the confined space for a source of the smell. Noticing her frantic search, Olen waved her over and pointed out the window. Down below the man-of-war, slowly creeping out of the mists, was the tip of an island. The air here was tinged a dirty brown, and Ana suddenly realized the smell of smoke was not coming from the gondola but rather from the foreboding landmass below.

Another tower, similar to the one at the port in Peju, slowly emerged from the smoky haze. The great jellyfish floated down gracefully and attached itself to the mooring post. Looking up at the bulbous air sac, Ana felt she could tell that the animal didn't want to be here any longer than absolutely necessary. The pilot of the vessel, a grouper-like fellow, stepped down from above and waddled over to the door. He opened it and leaned out of the craft, yanking on a rope to lower a gangway so that Ana and her companions could disembark.

Outside, the three adventurers were barely onto the platform before the door slammed shut, and the blimp departed with great haste off to the northwest, soaring up into the brownish-orange haze until it disappeared entirely from view.

"Well, here we are," said Olen with a matter-of-fact shrug. "Welcome to Port Arbalest."

Ana opened her mouth to speak, but the air she inhaled was so caustic she could only cough.

The three of them wandered down off the tower and up onto a small rocky shore. There were a handful of buildings here, simple cobblestone fortlike structures that seemed thrown together out of defensive necessity more than any particular architectural plan. A low wall encircled the whole village, but it was broken and smashed in many places. Indeed, the whole place seemed to be more a ruin than a functional port of call.

Olen pointed to the larger building up toward the woods, if the blackened trunks could be called such—the whole area had been reduced to cinders. "That used to be an inn of some sort. There's not much left, but there's bunks inside. By the stars though, this place looks even worse off than the last time I was here."

After walking over to a charred stump, he brushed off some of the ash and debris, and pulled a cylindrical leather map case out of his bag. He unsnapped the top, then laid the parchment down on the stump and unfurled it across the surface.

"We're here, in Port Arbalest," he said, pointing to the lower left-hand corner of the map. "And we've got to get to the Forge of Nightmares, here," he continued, gesturing to a large structure in the center. "And to do that, we've got to go up around these hills, through the ancient barrows, and then into the Everblaze. The forge is here, in the middle of the forest. I'd say, maybe ten miles in, ten miles back out again. If we're lucky, we can do it in one night and be back for the blimp tomorrow. If not …" Olen looked over at the dilapidated ruins up the shore.

Ana looked back and forth at her companions, soot already beginning to stain their faces and clothes.

"Are you sure you're really up for this?"

Sundry smiled. "Yes. And anyway, it's too late to turn back now. If we stay here, we'll probably get murdered by some wandering elemental."

"Agreed. So let's get a move on," said Olen as he stowed the map, slung his bag over his shoulder, and headed off into the blackened expanse.

*   *   *

The first hour or so was uneventful. Ana, Sundry, and Olen trudged through the charred shrubs and blackened stumps that had once comprised the forest east of Port Arbalest. Small hills took them up and down the landscape as flecks of grey ash fell like snow from above. From time to time, they would pass a ruined hut or a dried-up well, but any semblance of life had long since been driven out of this haunted place.

The silence here was deep—no birds in the trees, nor leaves to rustle back and forth in the hollow wind. Just the dull thud of footsteps upon the thick layer of soot covering the forest floor. Olen led the way, carefully picking a path through the colonnade of trees long since stripped bare by the lashing flames. Behind him, Ana and Sundry scanned the periphery for any signs of movement.

As the trio approached the remains of a low stone wall, there was a sudden rustling up ahead. Olen ducked down under the cover of the wall, and his companions followed suit. One by one, they cautiously peeked over the edge of the barricade. There, a few yards ahead, stood a scraggly-looking bundle of twigs and singed foliage. About its head flickered a faint, smoky black flame.

Slowly it bent down to pick up a rusted metal bucket. Then, step by stilted step, it staggered over to a nearby well. The wooden fixtures above the well had burned away, and there was no rope to which a bucket might be affixed. But the creature went through the motions just the same, dipping the bucket into the empty hole. There was an earnestness about its movements that reminded Ana of Gorthek, but there was also an emptiness, a pitiable melancholy that was almost difficult to watch.

"What's it doing?" Ana whispered.

"The elementals of this land are forever harried by the ghosts of the past who refuse to move on," said Olen. "At best, they are stuck, endlessly repeating the rituals that once brought them comfort in life. At worst, their anguish consumes them, and they spend their days sowing destruction across the land."

Having retrieved a bucketful of dust and ash, the creature slowly lumbered off into the woods, perhaps to tend the remains of some barren farm that had once lain nestled in a peaceful grove.

Olen rose to his feet once again, and his companions followed suit. As they set off again through the ruins, Ana crept up next to Olen.

"What happened to the people here?" she asked.

"No one really knows," he said. "A long time ago, something awful happened here. And now there's no one left who remembers what it was. We know from the ruins that there used to be a lot of people here, but somewhere along the way, they just … disappeared."

"That's crazy," said Ana. "How could a whole island's worth of people just up and vanish?"

"Yer guess is as good as mine, lass. But one thing's for sure: the three of us are the only living things on this forsaken rock today."

As the party continued on, the blasted trunks gradually began to thin out. As they crested the final hill, a great barren wasteland of thin, dark grass and burial mounds stretched out before them.

Here and there, huge stones jutted out of the ground, marking the resting place of some long-forgotten paragon. On the very hill upon which they stood, a half-decimated stone sat in several pieces on the ground. Ana walked up to it and rolled over a large chunk. On it were written runes or glyphs of some language she could not recognize, much less decipher.

"These graves belong to the people who lived on this land before the Disaster," said Olen as Sundry slung her bow down off her shoulder and drew an arrow from the quiver on her back. Carefully she nocked it, ready for a precision strike at a moment's notice.

"What language is this?" asked Ana. "What does it say?"

"I couldn't tell ye. None yet live who could decipher it."

Sundry scanned the horizon with a look of consternation upon her brow, then nodded to the dwarf, who took up his weapon and began to descend the hill into the great dead expanse.

Moving through the valleys between the rolling hills, Ana still felt horribly exposed. Though the sun was still high in the sky, she could not see it for the roiling dark clouds that seemed a permanent fixture over this desolate place. Periodically they would pass around a large round stone rolled into place against a hillside. No doubt on the other side of each was some tomb that had lain undisturbed for untold millennia.

Olen took point, his eyes close to the ground, ready to pounce on any threat. Sundry followed him, scanning the skies continuously, watching in every direction. Ana brought up the rear, Malthor's sword at the ready, its pommel giving out a steady glow as perhaps the only friendly light in the otherwise bleak and ruined plain.

Eventually, as the party weaved their way through the valleys, they came across a pile of boulders that seemed to have been strewn down from above. Next to the boulders was a gaping crater in the ground, perhaps where one of the burial mounds had been. It seemed to have exploded from within, sending rock and carrion into the surrounding area. Small bits of bone and scraps of cloth littered the ground around the eruption.

Lifting herself up over the boulders, Ana caught a glimpse of the ruined tomb. What remained of the inside was intricately detailed, the stone carved to resemble woven knots and other sorts of sophisticated designs. Of the barrow's former resident, however, there remained no trace.

For several hours, the group continued on. Occasionally they would pass a shattered stone or a ruined mound, but the going was otherwise silent and monotonous. The sky grew ever darker as the sun neared the horizon behind a thin sheet of roiling clouds.

But on the horizon, a fiery glow began to simmer. The stale, irritating haze of the coast was slowly replaced by the sharper, oilier scent of freshly charred wood.

As they wandered up the final hill, Ana looked back at the ghostly expanse behind her. The stones stood against the soot-stained sky as silent witnesses to a genocide no mortal was left to remember. Turning back to her companions, she stared now into the tumultuous, heaving glow of the Everblaze—the forest of eternal fire, kept burning by infernal elementals for ages beyond history.

"This is where it gets a wee bit exciting," said Olen as he entered the edge of the forest. "Stick close, and if ye see another one of those elementals, give 'em the business end of yer sword, eh?"

23

As they crossed into the wildfire, the blast of heat was immense. The air was impossibly dry, and filled with the choking scent of soot and charcoal. The team pressed on through the heat, Ana in front now, hacking away at the burning branches with her sword to cut a reasonably safe pathway through the fire.

Occasionally a great bang would echo through the forest as the sap inside a distant tree boiled, the internal pressure building up and exploding the tree from within. But Ana pressed on, Olen and Sundry following close behind, occasionally stopping to pat out small fires on each other's cloaks from wayward embers floating through the air.

As Ana continued to hack away at the flaming under-brush, suddenly she saw a strange and unnatural flickering in the distance. Two little fire elementals were playing chase around a tree, their small fiery bodies wreathed in some sort of dark, seditious flame. *Emberlings*, Ana recalled as she brought the sword up and motioned for Olen and Sundry to stop. But even as she paused to plan a way around the diminutive elementals, it was too late.

In a flash, they were upon her, jumping from tree to tree until they alighted on a fallen log just behind her, cutting her off from her allies. One of them leaped up and attempted to grapple her to the ground, while the other jumped at Olen. Ana swung out wildly with the sword, her arm engulfed in flames even as she cut straight through the creature. Something in her wild swing con-nected, and she could see the black tendrils wreathing the small creature snap and recede into nothingness. The fire flickered and faded, leaving the skin on her arm singed red from the assault.

Olen, meanwhile, had swung in with his maul, missing and connecting with a dead tree, which exploded into ash and embers at the impact. The emberling had sailed over his head and landed behind him, where it reared up for a second strike. But suddenly an arrow sailed into its fiery heart, severing the viscous, smoky strands of darkness and withering the creature into smoke and burnt grass.

"I owe ye one," said Olen as he turned to face Sundry.

"You alright?" she shouted back to Ana over the din of the crackling fires around them.

"Yeah, I'm good," she said, cradling her arm slightly. "Let's keep going."

They continued through the relentless barrage of heat and flame for some time until at last they emerged into a wide clearing. The burning forest forged a ring of fire around a monumental stone structure. It appeared to be almost templelike in its appearance. Two great stone spires rose up on either side, and between them, above the roof of the structure, was chained what appeared to be an enormous flame elemental, wreathed in black fire, struggling against its enchanted bonds.

"The Forge of Nightmares," said Olen. "Quick, let's get in there and get to work."

Above the stone-wrought doorway was a great face, contorted in anguish. A bas-relief depicting a great mass of tendrils extending up from the earth was carved into the stone behind it. As they crossed into the forge, the oppressive heat died down slightly, and the constant shrieking rage of the gigantic fire elemental above was reduced to a dull rumble by the thick stone walls.

In the center of the room was a massive obsidian altar, flecked with what appeared to be shining red dots—rubies, perhaps, embedded in its surface. Carved into the top of the altar were various channels—grooves in different shapes, sizes, and positions. A chain extended down from the ceiling and ended in a wicked-looking hook, from which hung a large stone crucible.

"These channels here," said Olen as he set the bag down and laid his hammer across the altar, "were meant for sacrifice. For blood. But today we're gonna use 'em for something a little less destructive—a little more creative."

Grasping the maul once again, he raised it up and hooked it into a groove at the top of the crucible. After lifting it off its hook, he brought it gently down and placed it on the altar.

"Sundry," he called out, "would ye be a dear and guard the door? I don't want any curious elementals coming in here and catching us with our proverbial pants down."

Sundry nodded and took up a defensive position by the entryway.

"Ana, I'd love your help over here while we cook up this fancy little necklace."

Ana sheathed her sword and walked over to join Olen by the altar as he brought the bag up to sit on the surface next to the empty crucible.

"Alright, first things first, let's get our lens together." Olen reached into the bag and pulled out a handful of small rocks, then handed them to Ana. "See my hammer over there? Chuck these into the crucible and pound 'em up real good, like."

Ana proceeded as instructed, rendering a fine batch of limestone powder in the base of the crucible. Meanwhile, Olen produced from his blacksmithing kit a small phial of tiny white crystals. He poured them into the crucible as well, then did the same with the jar of sand. Even in this hellish place, the subtle glow of the Sands of Time was strangely comforting.

"Alright, here comes the fun part." After placing the crucible back on the hook above the altar, he walked back to the rear wall and located the point at which the other end of the chain had been moored. He unwrapped it from a metal cleat attached to the wall, then pulled the chain, lifting the crucible upward steadily, a few feet at a time. "Ana! D'ye see that lever on the western wall?"

Ana looked over and nodded. "I do!"

"Go over there and give it a pull, would ye? And cover yer ears if ye can!"

Ana ran over to the large metal lever and heaved it down with all her strength. The rust and ash gave way, and it slid down into position with a thunderous clank. Suddenly it began to rain more ash and dust as a hidden mechanism in the roof of the forge ground to life. An opening in the ceiling slid to the side, revealing the writhing fire elemental above, and casting wildly hot flames down into the chamber below. The wailing and screeching was almost unbearable, but Olen continued to haul the payload up. It ascended through the hole on the chain and climbed up still farther, directly into the heart of the tortured emberling.

Dread seconds ticked by, one by one, until, after a few minutes, Olen let up the tension on the chain, and it came falling steadily back into the room.

"Ana! Close the gate!" he cried over the hellacious din.

With great effort, she pushed the lever back up, and the firestorm above died down once again to a dull roar.

As the bucket descended back into place over the altar, Ana could see even from where she was standing that the contents had become a glowing molten mass. Olen tied the bucket off once more and came back over to the altar, carefully scanning its surface for the appropriate nook.

"Aha!" he said. "It's this one right here, look." He pointed at a small circular indentation in the surface of the altar, about two and a half inches in diameter. It had a subtle curvature to it, as might the surface of a magnifying glass. Reaching up and carefully guiding his hammer along the bottom edge of the crucible, he tilted it forward slightly, and a stream of molten glass poured out and into the small disk. Even as it hit the mystical surface of the altar, it was already beginning to harden.

"That's job one done," Olen said, mostly to himself. "Now we make the setting."

As before, he rummaged through his bag, producing this time the small orichalcum figurines. Into the freshly empty crucible they went. Ana took the dagger and tossed it into the pot. *I hope this counts as a Relic of Life*, she thought to herself. Olen sprinkled in a handful of other powders and chemicals to aid in the process of extracting and burning off impurities. Then, up went the crucible, as before.

Ana once again manned the lever, and the tormented creature above scorched the crucible's contents with its boiling, eternal rage. As it descended back into the chamber, Olen this time selected a small doughnut-shaped depression and poured the molten mixture into the mold. As it was cooling and setting into shape, he extracted the now-finished glass lens. It glowed slightly, with the mysterious Sands of Time in its heart now lending their subtle magic to the crystal-clear eyepiece.

"Nearly there. We just have to wait for this setting to cool. Then we can mount the lens and get the hell out of here."

"We may need to get the hell out of here a little sooner than that, dear," came Sundry's voice by the door. "Something's coming this way. Something big."

24

As Olen was managing the slowly cooling setting, Ana ran over to Sundry's side. Sundry pointed over the charred grass to the edge of the blazing forest. Through the boiling, shifting air, she could just barely make out a large figure emerging from the flames. It seemed to be ten or twelve feet tall, moving slowly and wreathed in thick black smoke. Though it was still fairly far away, it was clearly heading straight for the forge.

Ana looked back at Olen, who was quickly but carefully polishing the now-cooled lens. The setting, however, still looked red-hot.

"How much time do you need?" she called back into the dim interior.

"Eight, maybe ten minutes?" Olen shouted back. "Can ye buy us a little time?"

Ana turned her attention back to the hulking creature slowly approaching from the woods. Placing a hand on the grip of her sword, she steeled her resolve and began to march back out into the clearing. Behind her, Sundry raised her weapon, bowstring taut and arrow trained on the approaching threat.

As Ana drew closer and closer, she realized the creature was hefting an enormous shield in its left hand. It glowed a fierce orange in the heat, as if perpetually on the verge of melting. In its right hand, it carried a giant flaming sword—the blade alone was at least as long as Ana was tall. It continued lumbering toward her, leaving a plume of smoke and ash in its wake.

The heat was growing ever fiercer, and Ana could scarcely maintain a grip on her sword for the sweat that was pouring down her palms. Now mere yards away from the beast of smoke and fire, she stopped, drew her blade, and held it aloft in a challenging pose, her body a vehement ultimatum: *You shall go no farther.*

"Halt, demon!" she cried.

To her surprise, the creature stopped. Its giant flaming sword rose up over its head and then came plummeting down, surging into the earth with a great crack of fire and brimstone. A deep, guttural laugh resounded throughout the clearing. Ana held her ground, blade held high in silent defiance.

The smoke shrouding the creature's appearance began to recede slightly, as though a cloak had been pulled back, revealing a black stone skull, almost like pumice, cracked in places, with red molten rock seeping through from underneath. The giant, oddly proportioned head was wreathed in flame, and the arms protruding from the smoke were skeletal in form.

"What?" he said. "You don't recognize me?"

Ana blinked, raising her left hand to wipe the sweat and ash from her eyes.

"Doro? Is that you?"

The imposing skeleton, cloaked in smoke and wrought of volcanic stone, pulled his white-hot shield aside and bowed deeply. "At your service, my dear."

Ana was struck by this sudden reappearance of her old friend. Immediately she sheathed her blade and stepped forward. Though the heat in the clearing was fierce, in his presence it receded somewhat.

"What are you doing on the Isle of Fear?" she asked.

"I live here," he said simply. "What are *you* doing on the Isle of Fear?"

"We're trying to craft the Periapt of Pursuit—the amulet that Olen thinks might help us find Amber."

"Aha! Excellent," said Doro as he turned to retrieve his sword. "So you met up with Olen, then. That's good news. And how did things turn out with Lady Sundry?"

"Come with me," said Ana, beaming. "I'll show you."

*　　*　　*

Through the smoke, the haze, and the shimmering heat, Sundry could scarcely make out the scene that was taking place in the clearing before her. She stood in the doorway of the forge, arrow trained on the large, shadowy creature.

Suddenly Ana turned around and began to walk back toward the forge, with the creature apparently in hot pursuit. Sundry drew back the bowstring, preparing to launch an arrow directly at this fearsome beast, when Ana called out. "Hey! Sundry! It's Doro!"

The tension on the bowstring slackened momentarily as she attempted to parse the situation.

The monster cloaked in black smoke raised his shield in greeting.

"It's good to see you again!" he called, striding up behind Ana. Sundry could now see his blackened visage, a deep-red glow of embers lighting up his strangely comforting eye sockets.

As Ana and Doro reached the entrance to the forge, Doro glanced up at the great emberling chained to the roof of the building.

"Poor soul," he said. "He has been here ever since the island fell, and he will stay here until it sinks into the sea." He looked down at Sundry, who had lowered her bow and now stood smiling up at him.

"I owe you a great debt," she said. "Without you, I would not be here today. Thank you."

"It was a team effort," said Doro, smiling down at Ana.

From inside the forge, Olen's voice rang out. "Ah, Doro, good to see ye! Yer just in time to find out if any of this nonsense worked or not."

Stepping around the altar and beckoning Ana forward, Olen unveiled his creation. It looked a bit like an oversize monocle. The device itself was comprised of a faintly glowing piece of sea glass, set inside a circular ring of brilliant orichalcum. Various indecipherable runes had etched their way into the piece, likely transferred from the altar, and the whole thing hung from a simple golden chain.

"Here," said Olen. "Give 'er a try."

Ana stepped forward, and Olen stood up on his tiptoes and gently lifted the necklace over Ana's bowed head. The periapt hung across the back of her neck and down over the front of her chiton. Immediately Ana was struck by how light it was—it felt almost weightless. Taking the lens in her hands, she held it up to her eye and peered through while Sundry, Doro, and Olen looked on expectantly.

The world on the other side of the lens seemed the same, if slightly dimmed by the glass's coloration.

"What do ye see?" asked Olen.

Holding it up and peering at her friends, she could not tell that anything was really different. There was Doro in his billowing cloak of black smoke, Sundry in her smart—if rather badly singed—leather armor, and Olen, looking up at her with tools in hand. She began to spin clockwise around the room, looking at the various designs on the walls, the altar, the ceiling—none of them looked particularly different. Ana sighed and returned her gaze to the door.

She was about to inform Olen that the experiment had failed when suddenly she noticed a faint glimmer in the periphery of the lens. Following it along to the northwest corner of the room, she realized that the glimmer was not something in the room but something in the far distance.

"I see something!" said Ana excitedly.

"What is it? What does it look like?" asked Olen.

"There's some sort of shining light over here. But it looks like it's not in this room. It's maybe far away. Maybe not even on this island."

"Let's have a look, hmm?" Olen walked over and gently gazed into the lens. "I'm not sure I see what yer talking about."

Taking back the amulet, Ana held it to her eye once again. The distant glimmer was gone.

"I swear it was just over there somewhere." She sighed, turning the device over in her hands.

"Mmm ..." said the dwarf. "Well, the book doesn't say much about how to actually use this thing, but if the Sands of Time are any indication, I'd say time is the key here."

"Indeed ... I wonder if we took it somewhere that we know Amber has been ... I wonder if we'd see anything then," said Sundry.

"Not a bad theory," said Doro with a nod, "but in any case, we should leave this place. Amber is most assuredly not here, and the Everblaze is growing more dangerous by the minute."

"Agreed," said Ana. "Let's get out of here."

The party made their way swiftly out of the great archway under the writhing emberling and ran for the western edge of the forest, leaving the Forge of Nightmares in the darkening haze behind them.

As they reached the raging inferno, a trio of tiny, crazed emberlings leaped out of the trees before them. Ana slid to a halt, brandishing her sword as they hopped around in a frantic dance.

"Get behind me!" shouted Doro as he strode up to meet the awful creatures. One of them jumped up and leaped clear over him to land behind—the other two met their end as his great blade swung clean through their tiny bodies. The survivor flew up onto Sundry, clambering all over her body as her armor smoked and caught fire. Jumping up into her, Olen tackled her to the ground, and the diminutive elemental rolled off into the ashen soil beside them. Before it could go any farther, Ana's sword swung down and snuffed it out, its blackened tendrils withering away into the dust.

"Ye alright?" asked Olen as he struggled to roll himself off the councillor.

"A little singed, but otherwise no worse for wear," she said, picking herself up off the ground. Her face was covered in ash and soot, and scorched holes were beginning to appear in her once pristine leather armor.

"Come on, there's no time to waste!" called Ana from the front.

She and Doro took the lead, hacking away at the underbrush and carving a path out through the choking flames. For what seemed like ages, they fought through the raging blaze, choking on thick smoke and dodging falling limbs from the desiccated trees above. At last, though, the fires died down a bit, and before long, they had come to the edge of the forest, back out on the fringe of the grey and barren mounds of death.

As they stepped past the last of the smoking tree stumps, Ana's joy at clearing the Everblaze turned suddenly to sickening dismay. There, on the horizon, cutting a dark silhouette against the slate-colored clouds, was the giant, hulking form of a creature she had hoped she would never see in person.

"Gravewalker," Sundry whispered, walking up behind Ana. "This just got a lot more difficult."

"We'll have to stay low," said Doro. "And quiet."

One by one, the adventurers crept down from the forest's edge, down into the valley between the two closest small hills. Even as they skirted the edge of the mounds, they could feel the heavy thud of the gravewalker in the distance, a shambling hulk looking for anything it could find to add to its collection. From standing stone to monument, they crept along, keeping just out of sight of the lumbering giant. But as they drew closer and closer to the decomposing tangle of moss and gravestones, its trajectory changed suddenly, and it doubled back toward their path.

"Quick, back. Get in behind that hill," hissed Olen under his breath.

Ana, Doro, Olen, and Sundry shuffled back as quietly as they could and slid behind a nearby burial mound. The rumbling thuds of the gravewalker's footfalls grew to a horrible crescendo as it approached. Doro was flattened against the side of the hill, his considerable height and smoking cloak a genuine disadvantage as the group attempted to maintain their stealth.

The gravewalker strode up and planted a massive stone foot just atop the mound under which the party was cowering. And for a few dread moments, there was only silence. Then came the crashing thud of another step as the gravewalker continued its search to the north.

Wordlessly Ana nodded at her companions, and one by one, they sneaked around to the opposite side of the hill, skirting the edges of the small valleys as best they could.

They were nearly back to the scorched remains of the forest outside Port Arbalest now. Just a few hundred yards more, and they could wave goodbye to this terrible place forever. The clouds were beginning to lighten, signifying the rise of the sun somewhere above the choking haze. Their ride would soon be returning from the islands beyond to take them back to Peju. It was in this moment of silent hope that the ground began to rumble beneath their feet.

"What the hell is that?" Olen whispered. "That gravewalker is a mile away by now."

A deep groan issued forth from the mound at Ana's feet. She had only moments to dive to the side as the entire hill erupted in a great explosion of rocks, charred grass, and human remains. Olen and Doro held up their shields to protect the team from the detritus pelting them from above as bones and sod rained back down to the earth.

Ana cursed under her breath as she crawled along the ground back to the relative safety of her companions. As the torrent of rocks and ash began to let up, Olen and Doro slowly lowered their shields. Gazing up into the sky, they saw a giant wall of rock and bone rise up before them.

Towering into the oily haze, a dark fire floated around the shattered grave, filling the newborn gravewalker with an insatiable hunger for carrion.

Ana, Sundry, and Olen stood paralyzed with fear. The gravewalker lurched forward and pulled one of its legs slowly up out of the freshly formed crater.

In an instant, Doro was on the move. "Run!" he cried, throwing himself in between the party and the titanic elemental. "I will buy you the time you need. Get to Port Arbalest!"

Sundry and Olen were already sprinting for the blackened tree line. Ana, however, was standing next to Doro as a great stone fist hurtled down from the sky, exploding into the ground next to them. Rearing up, Doro brought his flaming sword down upon the rocks, clattering with sparks, and small bits chipped off.

As the appendage soared back up into the sky, he turned once again to Ana. "You must get to the shore. I will handle this poor fellow."

"I won't leave you," said Ana. "You're coming with us."

"I can't," said Doro, with a tinge of sadness in his voice. "Get back to Istabar. Amber is counting on you. Finish your journey."

Turning back to the gravewalker, Doro raised his sword up into the heavens and shifted his weight back to brace himself against the remains of the mound.

"I am Doromondas, Shepherd of Fear!" he cried. "You will return to the earth from whence you came, gravewalker!"

The fist came down once more and connected with Doro's shield in a catastrophic explosion of fire and stone. Ana was once again thrown back, her shoulder connecting with the hard ground as she rolled across the soot-stained earth. Slowly she picked herself up off the barren valley floor and rose unsteadily to her feet. As the smoke and dust began to clear, Doro stood, seemingly unmoved by the incredible force of the impact.

He looked over at her and gazed silently for a moment. She nodded at him and began to back away toward the beach. Turning back to the elemental, Doro drew himself up and began to run toward the creature, sword ablaze. As Ana ran up the final hill and crossed into the blackened thicket, she turned to see Doro, still swinging, hope against hope, as the gargantuan gravewalker pummeled him with a flurry of blows from above.

Running back through the woods, she at last caught up with Sundry and Olen. At breakneck pace they retraced their steps, winding through the remains of the outskirts of Arbalest. At last they emerged on the other side of the low cobblestone wall. In the distance, a giant man-of-war was floating lazily down through the clouds and into the thick, caustic haze that blanketed the Isle of Fear.

"C'mon, we've got to get on board that blimp, or we're in serious trouble," said Olen.

The three adventurers vaulted over the low wall and ran for the small stone tower at the edge of the shore. The jellyfish extended its prodigiously long tendrils as the door to the gondola swung open. Spiraling up the stairs to the tower, Ana could see the hulking gravewalker approaching the town. It would be here in a matter of moments. After reaching the top of the platform, the three of them leaped aboard the vessel with such speed that the gangway slipped out of its moorings and fell, clattering to the ground below.

"Let's go, ye ruddy bastards! We've got a big, angry death monster out there, and it's gonna wear us all for jewelry if we don't get outta here right now!" Olen yelled as the dour-looking fish-person scuttled his way back up to the controls above the passenger area.

Slowly the tendrils unwrapped from the tower, and the man-of-war began its ascent away from the island. Ana watched with trepidation as the gravewalker crashed through the trees and lumbered toward the vessel. It was closing in on them with every giant, heaving step, but as the blimp began to pick up speed, the gravewalker began to crash out into the waves and sink down into the silt on the edge of the shore. Slowly it came to a halt, just out of reach of the airship.

There it stood as its prey floated off and away into the skies. Ana, Olen, and Sundry gazed out upon the pitiable mound of corpses as it faded away into the smoke and the haze, and at last disappeared under the clouds for good.

Ana slid back in her seat and heaved an enormous sigh of relief, though the elation of her escape was tempered by the uncertain fate of her dear friend.

Sensing her dismay, Sundry came to sit beside her. The rest of the patrons in the gondola gazed on in mild shock at this band of utterly disheveled, wounded ruffians.

"It's alright, Ana. He'll be okay."

"How do you know that? First Malthor's Mound, now the Isle of Fear. I've abandoned him twice now, and all he's ever done is look out for me."

"Doro is a Shepherd. He has lived for thousands of years. He will live for thousands more. He guides those in need of help, and you are in need of help. He will be alright."

Ana was dissatisfied with this answer, but in that moment, she was too exhausted and injured to press the matter any further.

As the dirigible continued to ascend through the clouds and back in the direction of the Isle of Hope, the rush of fresh, clear air into the cabin was a welcome change from the ever-present choking fumes of the past twenty-four hours.

As the ship glided effortlessly over the sea below, Ana found herself toying absentmindedly with the periapt around her neck. It seemed to be simply a small lens encased in a ring of metal. Was this really the key to finding Amber, or yet another red herring? She cradled it in her hands and gazed down into the indecipherable inscriptions molded into the orichalcum.

After some time, the jellyfish began to descend, and before long, Ana, Sundry, and Olen found themselves standing once again in the familiar streets of Peju.

"Entertaining as that was, that's not an adventure I'd like to repeat anytime soon," said Olen. "Still, we got what we came for."

"Let's head back to the city and get cleaned up," said Sundry, casting an empathetic eye toward Ana, who was clearly lost in the depths of despondency. "Then we can take a closer look at this periapt and see what it might have to show us."

"I like any plan that involves a good long shower and not wearing this blasted armor anymore," said Olen as he strode off toward the train station.

Sundry and Ana followed suit, and soon they were aboard the train and rolling off to Istabar once more.

25

Fluorescent lights flickered overhead, bathing the walls in a cool, sterile glow. As Ana navigated the labyrinth of hallways, she wondered what it could have been. Too many X-rays as a child? Too much fast food over the years? Too many hours in front of the microwave at work? Maybe it was just bad genes. It was all a roll of the dice, of course, but sometimes she wondered which die had finally come up wrong.

"Good evening." A voice at the nurses' station ahead interrupted her speculation. "Here to see Amber?"

Ana nodded.

After stepping around the desk, he walked past several doors and stopped at one on the left side of the hallway.

Ana followed in close pursuit. He knocked, then opened it without waiting for any response and motioned Ana into the room.

"Visiting hours are up at nine, just so you know," said the nurse to no one in particular as he was already on his way out the door again. Ana closed it gently behind him.

She crossed over to the left side of the bed, pulling a chair up from against the wall to sit next to her partner.

"Hey," said Ana.

"Hey." Amber smiled. Her skin was looking a lot better—maybe the best it'd looked in months now. Her cheeks were rosy, and her close-cropped hair was starting to fill in a little more. "How was the trip back home?"

"Oh, it was fine, I guess," said Ana. "My mom always makes things a million times more complicated than they need to be. Why can't we just get together for the holidays as a family? I don't know why it needs to be such a production."

"I think my parents were disappointed I couldn't make the trip out this year," said Amber. "But my brother flew all the way over from Halifax. It was really sweet of him."

"I saw the photos. Are you still planning on Alaska in the spring?"

"I hope so. I mean, it depends, obviously. But yeah."

Ana reached out to hold Amber's hand, and the two sat in silence for a moment, listening to the wall clock's second hand as it ticked through the night.

"You know, there's a bedpan under these sheets," said Amber, raising a mischievous eyebrow.

"Oh yeah?"

"I could be peeing right now, and you'd never know."

"I feel like I would know," said Ana. "I feel like that's something that would be evident."

"Well, there's only one way to find out."

"You're gross," said Ana.

"Your *face* is gross," came the rebuttal.

"I got you something." Ana reached down to her bag on the floor and pulled out two small parcels wrapped in tissue paper.

"Aw, you're so sweet," said Amber. Ana handed her the larger parcel first. It was rectangular in shape, and fairly heavy in Amber's wilted arms. Slowly she tore the paper off to reveal a book entitled *Star Trek Crosswords, Book 1.* "Yes!" Amber cried with glee. "This is the greatest gift anyone has ever given me. At last my encyclopedic knowledge of warp-field dynamics and Alpha Quadrant exobiology pays off."

"I found it in a used-book store down in Capitol Hill. It was mostly filled in, but I took an eraser and cleared out all the answers."

"Amazing. I'm going to go ham on this thing tomorrow. Maybe I'll have my own mini *Star Trek* marathon."

Setting the book down, Amber received the second parcel. Tearing off the paper revealed a small, squat square box. Amber pulled off the lid to reveal a stunning necklace. She gasped, pulling it up out of the box by its delicate golden chain. The pendant was a small gold setting, in which was set a brilliant drop of amber. There seemed to be bits of some kind of prehistoric insect trapped inside.

"Aw, amber!" she exclaimed.

"To add to your collection," said Ana, nodding.

"It's beautiful." Amber undid the clasp and tried to get it around her neck, but her reclined position on the bed and the wires and tubes attached to her hands made the maneuver challenging. Ana stood up and took the chain in her hands, carefully fastening it behind Amber's neck. The pendant dropped down onto her hospital gown and glittered in the pale fluorescent light.

"I love it. Thank you."

Standing over the bed, Ana lowered her head down to rest it on Amber's chest. For a moment, they shared a quiet embrace. Then a knock came once again at the door.

"Looks like time's up," said Ana as she slowly straightened up. Amber's arms slid across Ana's shoulders and then down her arms until she held Ana's hands in her own.

"I love you," Amber whispered.

"I love you too," said Ana, squeezing Amber's hands as she stepped away from the bed and picked her bag up off the floor. "I'll see you this weekend, right? We're gonna do MST3K night at Cinebarre?"

"You betcha." Amber smiled.

As Ana closed the door and began to walk back past the nurses' station, the sound of muffled singing blossomed into the hallway.

In the not too distant future,
Somewhere in time and space …

*   *   *

Ana awoke from her second night in Sundry's guesthouse. Slowly she unraveled the bandages on her arm to check on the burns. Whatever salve the mystic healers of Istabar had applied the evening prior, it had already dramatically improved the wounds. Even the cuts and scrapes on her face and body were showing signs of healing.

But despite the many hours of deep sleep, she still felt exhausted—drained. Perhaps the stress of her latest adventures was more than her body was really prepared for. Rolling out of bed, she realized she was still wearing the Periapt of Pursuit. Perhaps Olen was right—perhaps there was still another piece of the puzzle to be solved for the trinket to realize its utility. Or perhaps it was a failed experiment, sending them all on the latest fool's errand.

Throwing on her sky-blue garb, she made her way out, over the small bridge connecting the guesthouse to the main residence, and down into the gardens below, where Sundry was busy tending to the flowers.

"Ah, good morning. I trust you slept well—we have a busy day ahead of us. Olen asked us to meet him back at the Anvil as soon as you're ready."

Ana brushed the hair out of her face and steeled her resolve. "Let's get going."

*   *   *

"Alright, hear me out," Olen began as he paced around his office in the depths of the Anvil. "The recipe called for the Sands of Time. So I'm thinking time is a relevant piece of the puzzle. Maybe we have to use it at a particular time of day. Or maybe ye can only use it so many times before it stops working."

"Is there anything special about the orichalcum?" asked Ana.

"Well, it's a magical sort of metal. And certainly, it's rare. But I don't know that it has properties beyond bein' generally magical and rare."

"We combined it with the dagger," said Sundry. "In theory, that attuned the periapt to Amber."

"In theory, yes," said Olen. "But what that actually means, I have no idea."

Ana stood, leaning against Olen's desk, gazing down at the small amulet in her hands.

Suddenly she jumped up with inspiration. "I've got an idea." Turning to Olen, she asked, "Amber bought the dagger from one of your armorers, right?"

"Yes. According to the court testimony, Mr. Ian Woon sold her the dagger in the marketplace some several weeks back."

"Do you know specifically which stall?"

"Well, the Anvil maintains a set of stalls towards the northern part of the market. My guess would be in that direction—but the market's not on today, and Mr. Woon is likely at home."

"That's alright. Can you take me there?"

"Of course. It's just a short walk from here."

Ana practically ran up the stairs, through the hallowed halls of the Anvil, and out onto the streets of Istabar. As she made her way out of the crafting district and around to the marketplace by the Westward Gate, her eyes hunted around for the stalls in question.

"Over here!" Olen called as he moved through the crowd. Although the market was not on, the streets were still full of people on all manner of midmorning excursions. After pointing at a small group of stalls under a large awning decorated with an Anvil, Olen ducked around behind and searched about for a moment.

"Aye, these are the ones he'd have been selling at, but as I said, there's nothing to be found here today."

"Not today, no," said Ana, holding the shimmering sea glass lens up to her eye. She moved her field of vision from one empty stall to the next as pedestrians in the street filtered past. Suddenly she stopped with a gasp. There, standing at the furthest stall, framed by a ring of enchanted orichalcum, was Amber.

She was wearing a simple sundress, browsing the wares, her unmistakable curly blond hair shifting back and forth in a gentle breeze. She seemed to be speaking to someone, but there was no one on the other side of the table. Chancing a glance around the lens, Ana confirmed her suspicions. Amber was not standing on the street today. But she had been haggling with a merchant at this very counter in the past, and she could see it now, filtered through the Sands of Time.

"I can see her!" Ana shouted, beckoning her companions over with a free hand. She didn't dare take her eyes off the scene unfolding within the periapt.

"Well, I'll be damned," said Olen as he and Sundry looked on over Ana's shoulder.

Within the lens, Amber appeared to be haggling back and forth with Mr. Woon, though his image was not present in the frame. Ana couldn't hear any of the dialogue, but a transaction was clearly taking place. She slowly strode forward, seeking a closer view of the exchange. Holding out her hand, Amber seemed to be depositing some coins on the desk, but they promptly vanished as soon as they left her grip. She reached out with her other hand and closed it gently, and the sinister weapon of Sundry's earlier demise, the barbed dagger, popped into her closed fist.

She inspected the blade thoughtfully for a moment, then slipped it into her belt and began to wander off into the crowd, her ethereal form clipping through the various real-world denizens of Istabar. As she took her next step, suddenly she vanished.

Ana spun the lens around wildly, trying to locate her image again, but it seemed the interaction was over.

"I think that might be all we get here," said Ana, furrowing her brow. "But at least now we know how this thing works."

"It may or may not show us where she is now," said Sundry, "but it seems like it can show us where she was."

"And that could be our ticket to figuring out where she went after she left the city," added Olen.

Sundry brought a hand to her chin in contemplation. "But if we can't follow her, how are we going to figure out where she went next?"

"Well, we know she lost the dagger at some point, and we know who found it," said Ana.

"Aye," said Olen. "And I've a sneaking suspicion it wasn't found by accident."

26

Captain Charles sat at his desk, high in one of the spires that marked the corners of the prison's imposing facade. Carefully he turned over a page in his paws—it was a letter from Lord Various Quinn, requesting the release of Ras Dashen, stating that he did not believe the creature was involved in the matter of Lady Sundry's death. Certainly, this missive would be admissible as evidence in Ras Dashen's trial, given the now-public knowledge of Various's betrayal and subsequent demise at the hands of his victim—his wife.

Charles filed the document away and turned back to his work as he heard a knock at the door.

"Come in," he said in reply. In through the door walked Olen, Ana, and Sundry. "Ah, my friends," he continued warmly, rising from his seat and stepping out from behind the desk. "So good to see you all alive and well. When I heard you were headed off to the Isle of Fear, I admit I feared the worst."

"I appreciate your concern, Captain," said Ana. "It wasn't a terribly comfortable trip, but we managed to accomplish what we set out to do." She slipped her hand under the amulet on her sternum and held it aloft for Charles's inspection.

"That is quite the trinket," he said, gazing critically into its shimmering lens. "I trust this means you've secured the answer to tracking down your friend Amber."

"We have indeed!" said Olen. "And quite a powerful little thing it is too."

"Then what, may I ask, brings you to my humble office this afternoon when you should be off locating your dear friend?"

"Well, that's just it," said Ana. "The periapt seems to show us what she was doing in certain places at certain points in time. But it doesn't seem like it'll show us where she is now. We know the dagger left her possession at some point, because Ras Dashen had it when he stabbed Lady Sundry. So I'd like to talk to Ras Dashen and find out how he got the dagger."

At this, Charles frowned—at any rate, as much as a basset hound can be said to frown. "Much as I would like to facilitate this meeting for you, I fear access to Ras Dashen will be difficult. His trial is tomorrow, and he has been moved to a cell under the Tower of Drasz until he appears on the stand in the morning."

Ana slumped back against the wall, her arms folded across her chest.

"I do have good news, however," Charles continued. "We know how he came to possess the dagger. Once we told Ras Dashen about Lady Sundry's return and the mounting pile of evidence against him, he became a lot more cooperative—I suspect in hopes of a more lenient sentence.

"After a great deal of further interrogation, we've discovered he paid Amber to acquire it for him. Much in the same way that he feigned distress to lure you into the company of Lord and Lady Quinn, he similarly promised a courier's fee to Amber in exchange for her retrieval of the dagger. It seems he sought a layer of plausible deniability between himself and the murder weapon, and Amber— being a fresh visitor to the city—needed some coin of the realm. For what purpose, she apparently did not say."

"And do you know where this exchange took place? I mean, specifically where?" asked Ana.

"Let me check my notes," said Charles, taking a seat once again at his desk and pulling out a voluminous folder labeled "Quinn, Sundry." After flipping through page after page of hand-taken testimony, he at last appeared to locate what he was looking for. "Several weeks ago ... Amber of Seattle ... Woon's dagger ... A few days after she had purchased the dagger from Mr. Woon, Ras Dashen located her in a restaurant called the Blue Dragon, in the theater district. She gave the dagger to him, and he paid her the promised courier's fee."

"Does Ras Dashen mention her at all anywhere else?"

"I'm afraid not. That's the only part of his story that relates to your friend," said Charles.

"That's okay. We've got the information we need. Thank you, Charles!" said Ana as she headed for the door.

"Ana," Charles called out after her.

She paused at the threshold of his office and looked back.

"I do wish you the best of luck in locating Amber. If there's anything I can do to aid you in your search, I hope you will let me know."

"You've been a great help, Captain," she said, smiling. "Make sure Ras Dashen gets what's coming to him. We'll handle Amber. For the first time since I got here, I feel like we might actually be close."

With that, she disappeared through the door, Olen and Sundry hot on her heels as she rushed down the stairs and out into the street.

*   *   *

Despite the bright sunlight outside, the interior of the Blue Dragon was dark and melodramatic. Swirling blue lamps and art deco fixtures emphasized its mid-1920s aesthetic. The tables were ensconced in lavish booths upholstered in blue velvet, and the bar was right out of a Parisian dive.

Bottles of absinthe bleue and curaçao liqueur lined the mirrored backdrop.

The place was empty save for a handful of patrons languishing at the bar. The bar itself seemed untended, but Ana doubted their presence had gone wholly unnoticed. Raising the periapt to her eye, she began to scan the room.

Sure enough, the image of Amber flickered into view in a corner booth by the door. She was staring off into space, in quiet contemplation—listening to music that Ana could not hear, perhaps.

Ana slid into the booth next to her, carefully, keeping her eyepiece trained on the young woman, her curls bouncing lightly to some distant jazz rhythm. Reaching out, Ana's hand crept toward Amber's on the table. Gently Ana tried to grasp it, but her fingers only slid through and landed on the cold tabletop. She knew, of course. But it couldn't hurt to try anyway.

Suddenly something stole Amber's attention. Someone had joined her at the booth, opposite her position. They were not included in the lens's purview, but she was having some brief conversation with them. Slowly, furtively, she produced the dagger from her belt and slid it across the table. As soon as it left her grip, it was gone. In return, a small bag of coins was deposited, materializing in her hands. She weighed it in her hands quietly, gazing back off toward the band as Ras Dashen departed. Ana noticed that under the bag of coins was a train ticket. As the silent song reached its conclusion, she faded away, and Ana was left sitting alone once again as Olen and Sundry looked on.

"Well?" asked Olen. "What's the story?"

"It looks like she gave the dagger to Ras Dashen in return for some money and a train ticket, but I couldn't make out where the ticket was headed to."

"Well, that's easy enough to figure out," said Sundry. "Let's get on the train and see where she gets off."

* * *

As the train was rumbling along, Ana held up the periapt, scanning along the length of their car, hoping to catch a glimpse of Amber. But it seemed as though the trinket had little to say about Amber's trip out of Istabar. Fields, trees, and small homes passed by, and Ana once again thought of Doro. *When this is all over*, she thought, *I'm going to track him down too.*

After some time, the train began to slow as it pulled into the first stop on its journey, the fishing village of Peju. Stepping out onto the platform, Ana held up the periapt. To her surprise, she spotted Amber's ghostly figure stepping out of an adjacent car onto the platform, smoothing her dress and starting off down into the station until she promptly disappeared. Waving back to her companions, Ana hopped down off the platform and ran into the station, looking for any sign of Amber.

As Sundry and Olen joined her, they began to walk down the road while Ana held the amulet at eye level. Down they walked through the market stalls, passing all manner of dogs, cats, people, and fish until they arrived at the end of the boulevard, down by the harbormaster's office once again. Just as Ana was considering giving up her brute-force approach, Amber flickered once again into the frame of the lens. She was standing at the window of the harbormaster's office. After producing the bag of coins she had received from Ras Dashen, she placed it on the counter, where it promptly vanished.

Ana crept up behind the image of Amber, gazing down at the otherwise empty window as she waited for the ticket to be produced. Soon enough, Amber stretched out her hand and touched a piece of paper. As it blossomed into the lens, Ana made note of its destination. And no sooner had it appeared than Amber took it up and placed it in her pocket. She nodded a thank-you to the ticket vendor and wandered down toward the pier in the general direction of the jellyfish blimp, slowly fading out of sight and out of the amulet's perception.

"Any clues?" asked Olen.

"Yes. She bought a ticket for the jellyfish," said Ana.

Sundry crossed her arms. "Where to?"

"The Isle of Truth."

27

As the trio waited on the pier, the great silvery crest of the man-of-war faded into view through Peju's evening fog. Down the coast to the west, the sun began to sink below the horizon, lighting up the sky in a brilliant pink hue as low clouds cast deep shadows on their brethren higher up in the troposphere. Sundry's graceful blond hair shifted in the wind as cooler air from the ocean washed over the shore, wrapping the buildings and towers of Peju in a quiet blanket of mist.

"Looks like this is yer ride," said Olen, looking up at Ana as she stared off into the ocean. He took a deep breath and held out his arms for a hug. Ana turned and bent down to hold him in a tight embrace. "Like I said before, the Isle of Truth is … a solo experience. Much as we'd like to go with ye, I'm afraid yer gonna have to track her down on yer own from here on out."

"Thank you so much, Olen. For everything."

"It was a pleasure, lass. It really was. I haven't had an adventure like that in years."

"When I come back with Amber, you can have the periapt. It is your handiwork, after all."

Olen laughed. "Aw, that's real sweet of ye, dear, but that trinket is yers, and yers alone."

As Ana stood up, she turned to Sundry, who stood silently. Her lips were pursed, but her misty eyes betrayed the emotion caught in her throat.

"I wish we could go with you, Ana, and see this through to the end," she said. "But as you'll discover when you get on that blimp, we can't."

Ana nodded. In her heart, she knew this was farewell, though she did not understand why.

"And at any rate," Sundry continued, "we've got a trial to deal with tomorrow morning."

"And since the woman he's accused of murdering is here in the flesh to testify against him, I'd say it's a pretty open-and-shut case!" Olen laughed.

Ana and Sundry held one another close as the jelly-fish above them floated gently down toward the mooring tower. As the gondola door opened and passengers began to file out, Sundry released her grip on Ana and stepped back.

"I owe you my life, Ana, and I'll never forget that. When you get back here with Amber, I hope you'll both come to stay with us in Istabar for a while."

"I'd like that very much, and I'm sure she would too," said Ana. "You both have helped me so much. I'll be thrilled for you to meet Amber when we get back."

The boarding bell began to clang above. Ana took a deep breath as she turned and began to head toward the staircase that spiraled its way up the tower. Every step up that stairway felt to her like a thousand miles, but every fiber of her being whispered that the end was close at hand. As she reached the platform at the top, enshrouded in the sun-warmed mists, she took one last look at her traveling companions. They were waving from the ground. She waved back, smiling, then turned and entered the gondola.

There were a handful of other patrons on board as the door closed. Gently the jellyfish released its hold on the mooring tower and glided once again up into the skies above Peju. Farther and farther out to sea they flew, and Peju soon disappeared into the fog and the dying light as the world outside the gondola fell away into darkness.

With nothing left to see outside, Ana looked down to gaze at the Periapt of Pursuit around her neck. She held it up to her eye and looked around the cabin, but it seemed it had nothing to say about Amber's trip to the Isle of Truth.

As the minutes turned into hours, Ana sat in silence, save for the quiet whispers of the air flowing past the cabin. She closed her eyes and slumped back on the padded bench. In her mind's eye, she could still see the ethereal image of Amber as she sat in the Blue Dragon, tapping her fingers to an imperceptible melody.

*　　*　　*

Ana opened her eyes with a start. She was alone in the gondola, and it was no longer moving. She rose from her bench and walked over to the window to see the tendrils of the jellyfish wrapped securely around a graceful wrought-iron post. Unlike the port at Peju, the ground outside appeared to be level with the gondola, suggesting a cliff or some other precipitous drop-off, down into which the rest of the creature's tendrils were dangling. Looking back to the doorway, she found that it was open, though the conductor of the vehicle was nowhere in sight. Slowly she crossed the small cabin and stepped out onto the gangway.

Holding tight to the rails on either side, she made her way across the short metal plank. It was rather Gothic looking, and similarly graceful in its design to the mooring pole on the cliff face beside it. When she reached the other side, she found herself standing on hard stone. Looking back, she saw that the jellyfish was indeed floating against the side of the cliff. Slowly its tendrils unraveled from the post and slid off into the sea of clouds below. The gondola pulled away from its dock as the large, bulbous prow of the man-of-war swung away and began to glide down through the clouds and out of sight.

Wherever she was, she was alone.

It was quite dark, though a full moon illuminated the surrounding landscape. The immediate environment consisted of a rocky cliff face, bordered on one side by a sheer drop into a sea of billowy clouds. On the other side, a large stone wall rose up from the platform upon which she stood. A set of metal stairs led up to the top of the wall, beyond which she could not see. At the foot of the stairs was an intricate iron archway. On its sides hung two small glowing orbs—lamps of some sort. Across the top of the archway was inscribed, in ornate letters, "Welcome to the Isle of Truth."

Seeing nowhere to go but up, Ana grabbed her sword in its sheath, and the gem in its pommel sprang to life, casting a cool glow out over the cliffside and mingling with the melancholy wash of silver-blue moonlight from above. Passing under the iron archway, she gripped the railing and began to ascend the stairs. As her vantage point continued to rise, she could see that the ocean of clouds stretched out to the horizon, though in spots she could now see the gentle ocean shimmering far underneath. Beyond the sound of her sandals on the cool metal steps and the bluster of the wind, she was surrounded by silence on all sides.

Cresting the top of the stairs, she emerged upon a tremendous concrete expanse. It seemed to extend into the distance for miles, but on the horizon, she saw the familiar skyline of Seattle. As she stepped onto the concrete, she could scarcely believe her eyes. Glancing backward, she saw only clouds as far as the eye could see. And yet, up ahead, the glittering buildings and distant streetlights of Seattle rose up out of the ground and stretched into the midnight air above, skyscraper silhouettes backlit by deep-blue clouds.

As she began to walk toward the city, she heard a familiar voice behind her. "I love the city lights at night. They are truly beautiful, don't you think?"

Ana turned around to find a large skull smiling back at her. The bone was pristine ivory white; no fringing of kelp or cracks of molten stone could be seen. His robe was an incredible midnight blue, flecked with tiny points of light that twinkled and shifted as the wind moved gently across the fabric. Galaxies of brilliant purple and pink sprawled across the canvas even as comets flung themselves with reckless abandon through the void between the stars. In his hand, he held an enormous scythe of ebony with a gleaming steel blade.

"Doro," Ana said softly, "I'm sorry for what happened on the Isle of Fear. I didn't want to leave you, but I didn't have any other choice."

Doro laughed. "Few people ever choose fear. To face that fear, and brook the unknown, is to stand in the face of your own obliteration. You chose fear when you stepped onto that barren shore, and now you must decide whether to face the unknown once more."

"I'm not sure I understand," said Ana, imploring an elaboration from the Shepherd.

"Why don't we walk into the city together?" said Doro as he stepped forward and set off toward the skyline in the distance.

Ana nodded and walked up to follow closely at his side.

*   *   *

The streets of downtown Seattle were strangely devoid of any traffic. The sidewalks were empty, and not a single plane could be seen flickering through the skies. Ana and Doro walked right up the middle of the road, passing storefronts and offices on either side. Some of the lights were on, but there were no occupants to be seen.

"You came to the Midnight Beach looking for someone," said Doro. "Why did you come here?"

Ana thought for a moment. "I'm not sure. I knew she came this way. I figured it'd be easy to find her here, but I didn't realize what a large and complicated place this is."

Doro nodded. "But *why* did you come looking for her here?"

"I guess I was afraid I would never see her again."

"A valid fear," said Doro. "So what kept you from facing that fear?"

Ana crossed her arms, thinking back to the day she had arrived at the Midnight Beach. "I thought she needed my help."

"Did she?"

Ana looked down at the periapt around her neck. She stopped in the street and held it up to her eye. Just as in the Forge of Nightmares, there was a slight glimmer in the distance, but this time, the shimmering golden light felt closer—brighter than before, and somehow a little more tangible.

Breaking into a sprint, she began to run down the road. Doro followed, keeping up at a moderate pace with his deep and lengthy strides. The butt of his scythe clanked on the asphalt as he moved along the otherwise silent avenue. In the distance, a hospital rose up into the deep-blue night sky. As Ana neared the building, most of the windows were dark. However, a golden light was streaming out of one room on the top floor. Jogging in through the main entryway, Ana hit the call button for the elevator and waited as Doro strode up behind her.

After ducking into the elevator, he stood hunched over as the doors closed behind them. The floors floated by, one after another, until the doors opened onto the oncology ward. Stepping out, they made their way through the labyrinthine hallways until at last they arrived at a room. The door was closed, but light was streaming out from the jamb. Slowly Ana pushed it open.

Inside the room was a hospital bed. The window looked out onto the city streets below. There was a *Star Trek*–themed crossword book on the end table adjacent to the bed, and various machines, all disconnected and shut down. The bed itself was neatly made but empty. Ana walked numbly into the room and flopped backward onto the hospital bed, covering her face with her hands and pressing on her eyes in silent frustration.

"I really thought she'd be here," she said at last.

Doro ducked in through the doorway, then leaned his scythe up against the wall and knelt down, sitting cross-legged on the hospital floor. After a few silent moments, he spoke.

"A long time ago, there was a cult called the Servants of Disaster. They went to the Isle of Fear and tried to summon forth a horrible creature. Few now remember the details. But I remember. I was there."

Ana uncovered her face and looked over at the giant, oddly proportioned skeleton sitting on the floor.

"It was then the Isle of Wonder. And it was called such until the great Dys Hastur set foot upon its shores. This event has long been lost to the mists of time, but it is not because the people of Wonder were killed, nor because they did not share their story. It is because those who survived could not bear the pain of memory—the knowledge that life was once different. To choose fear was to choose madness.

"Even now, the tendrils of that long-forgotten disaster poison the land and rip the very rocks and trees asunder against the weight of their own anguish."

"Why don't they just stop fighting?" asked Ana.

"Because to face such a fear now would be to consign oneself to oblivion. An eternity of strife is preferable to the truth: that the halcyon days of Wonder are not ahead, but behind."

Ana sat on the bed, hands in her lap. She reached over and picked up the crossword book—it was mostly complete, except for a few pages here and there. The necklace, however, with its delicate amber pendant, was nowhere to be found.

"What do you do in the face of a truth that's too painful to bear?"

"I cannot answer that question for you," said Doro. "But this is the Isle of Truth. If it is truth you seek, you will find it here. What you do with that truth is up to you."

Doro rose, slowly, and turned to retrieve his scythe from the corner. Ducking back under the doorframe, he turned and looked again at Ana, who was still seated on the bed.

"Amber is here," he stated. "She is in the apartment that the two of you share. If you look at your periapt, it will guide you there."

Ana pulled out the trinket and held it to her eye, scanning around the room. Indeed, a bright glowing star settled into the frame as she held it to the northwest. It was below her, close to the ground, and tracked off in the direction of her neighborhood. Looking back at Doro, she saw he had straightened up on the other side of the door.

"The truth you seek is here," he said again. "Consider the fear behind that truth, and the oblivion behind that fear."

"Goodbye, Doro," said Ana. "I hope I see you again."

"I, too, hope that our paths will cross again before my time is done," said Doro. "Good luck."

With that, he continued down the hall and into the dark maze of corridors beyond.

Ana sat on the bed, periapt in hand, playing Doro's words over and over again in her mind. She picked up the crossword book once more, flipping through its pages from back to front. As the paper fluttered by, her thumb caught on the back of the front cover, and there was a note written there. It was unmistakably Amber's handwriting, a flowing cursive that seemed to exude special care on each delicate ligature.

Dear Ana,

I hope you know how much you mean to me. I'm sorry I couldn't make it to the movies with you this weekend. But maybe there could be a Netflix date in our future. They have all of The Next Generation, but we could skip the first season, since it does kind of suck.

Anyway, I love you. Please tell my parents and my brother that I love them too.

It was signed with her signature and a small heart. Placing the book back on the nightstand, Ana stood from the bed and walked out of the room. Her heart was racing, but she stood stock-still as the elevator returned her to the reception area. Stepping out into the street, deep-blue clouds billowing silently above, she began to make her way up the road toward the apartment.

Many blocks passed, but her firm resolve took her past darkened buildings and empty facades until at last she turned down a residential street and came up to the small apartment in which she and Amber lived. Once again she brought the periapt to her eye. There, just inside the building, up on the top floor, was a silhouette, rendered in shining golden light. It seemed to be seated, perhaps at the kitchen table, where they had shared so many quiet suppers together, or on the couch in front of the television.

She crossed the threshold and ascended the exterior steps up onto the unit's porch. Taking hold of the doorknob, she twisted it, swinging it open. The hallway inside was dark, but she navigated it with an almost unconscious fluency. Her feet took her up several flights of stairs and down a long, dark hallway, until at last she stood outside the door to the apartment.

Drawing in a deep breath, she placed her hand on the doorknob. She turned it, clockwise. It was unlocked. Gently she pushed the door open.

There, sitting at the kitchen table, was Amber.

28

Looking up from her book, Amber smiled.

"Hey, love," she said, placing the novel down on the table and sliding back her chair to stand.

Her beautiful blond hair fell down in tumbling curls across her shoulders. Even outside the periapt's lens, she possessed a sort of radiance that rendered her in vivid color, a stark contrast to the pale walls of the kitchen. She was still wearing the simple patterned sundress Ana had witnessed in the amulet's visions. Around her neck was the amber necklace Ana had gifted her in the hospital.

Amber walked around the table lightly and crossed the room to the door, holding out her hands for a hug. Stepping forward, Ana reached out to touch her open palms, still half expecting to fall right through them. But as her thumbs connected with Amber's hands, Ana felt the heat of Amber's gentle fingers close around hers. Amber pulled Ana's arms behind her back and then wrapped her arms across Ana's shoulders, sealing a tight embrace. Her chin rested lightly on Ana's shoulder as the two women held each other silently in the dimly lit kitchen.

Ana breathed in deeply, taking in the scent of her partner's vanilla shampoo. Tears began to streak down her face as she rocked back and forth against the wooden floor, squeezing Amber ever more tightly—afraid to let go.

After another few moments, she released her grip and stepped back, taking up Amber's hands once again and staring into her partner's eyes.

"I thought I'd never see you again," said Ana, her voice cracking slightly through the tears.

"Well, I was pretty much imprisoned in that hospital," said Amber, laughing. "It's not like you didn't know where to find me."

"I mean when you disappeared. I didn't know where you went. And I felt so awful that I wasn't there for you."

Amber's smile was warm as she grasped Ana's hands a little tighter and guided her across the kitchen and into the apartment's small living room. She led her to the well-worn couch, where the two sat next to one another. Amber put her arm across Ana's shoulders as Ana laid her head on Amber's chest.

"You knew where I went," said Amber. "Otherwise, you wouldn't have found me here."

"It's been a crazy journey. I almost didn't make it."

Ana told Amber about her travels—arriving at the Midnight Beach, meeting Doro, Ras Dashen, and Lord Various. Lady Sundry's murder, and her escape from Istabar. She told her of Malthor's Mound, the fishing village of Peju, and the trial. Amber listened intently as Ana detailed her battle with Various and her exoneration at the hands of a reborn Lady Sundry, and the quest for the Periapt of Pursuit that she now wore proudly around her neck.

"All of this," said Ana, "in the hopes that I'd see you again." Ana paused, her voice quivering as she sought for the right words. "When … when you died, I felt like I'd lost everything. I was afraid. I didn't know what to do."

"I love you, Ana," said Amber. "I always will. But I can't come home with you. I've found my own truth. And maybe someday we'll be here together, but I hope it's not today."

Ana looked up into Amber's eyes. Amber sighed and patted Ana's leg gently as she rose from the couch. She held out her hand, and Ana took it, standing from the sofa and following her back out to the kitchen. The two proceeded around the corner to the hallway.

As Ana rounded the corner behind Amber, she gasped. There, standing stationary in the hallway as if frozen in time, was a man in a firefighter's outfit, ax in hand. He seemed to be in midstride, barreling down the corridor on the way to somewhere.

"It's too late for me," said Amber as she carefully sidestepped the firefighter, "but it's not too late for you."

As Ana stepped around the man, she could see that in fact he was not frozen, but his movements were so slow as to be almost imperceptible. As her attention turned away from the man in the hallway, she saw that the door to the bathroom had been smashed in. Indeed, splinters and sawdust floated past her as she moved down the hall, suspended in the air like bubbles on still water.

Amber walked past the door to the bathroom and gestured inward. Ana rounded the corner and gazed into the small room. On the floor, a man and a woman in blue-and-yellow EMT uniforms were busy unpacking some sort of bag. Their movements, too, were like molasses. They seemed to be communicating fervently, but the timescale was much too slow to determine what they were talking about. Then her eyes fell upon the tub.

There, in the water, she saw herself. She was naked, her hair floating gently atop the surface. Her face was porcelain white, a stark contrast to the deep-crimson fluid in which she was submerged. She seemed to be asleep—oblivious to the flurry of activity occurring in slow motion around her.

"I know you were afraid," came Amber's voice from the hall. "I was afraid too. But I didn't have a choice. You did. You still do. But not for long."

Gazing out of the window, Ana could barely see the city lights. The skyline was dim now, and darkness encroached upon the small apartment, swallowing up the hospital, the trees, and the fence posts just outside.

Ana turned back to her partner, who was still standing patiently, framed by the door to the bathroom.

"I came here for you. I'm not leaving without you."

"Then you're not leaving," said Amber. "But I promise you, if you stay, you'll regret it."

"I'd rather be with you than out there by myself." Ana gestured to the window, which now framed nothing but a black void.

"I'll wait," said Amber. "No matter how long it takes, I'll wait for you."

Ana stepped toward the young woman in the doorframe. Down the hall, the lights flickered into darkness. The kitchen faded into the night. Even Amber, whose radiance brought such a warm and vivid joy to this gloaming space, was beginning to fade.

Reaching out once more, Ana took Amber's hands and leaned in, pressing her lips against those of her cherished love. For a moment, time stood still, and the darkness was content to wait.

On the floor, the paramedics were preparing to lift the body out of the tub. Down the hall, a stretcher was now on its way. Ana stood in the doorframe.

She took a deep breath, closed her eyes, squeezed Amber's hand, and let go.

Acknowledgments

I've heard it said that it takes a village to raise a child, and it seems to me the same may be true for many acts of creation, books included. No one writes in a vacuum—save, perhaps, authors of physics textbooks (that's why they're all non-friction). This book has been a team effort, and I'd like to recognize a few people who have helped bring it, kicking and screaming, into the world.

Shannon Roberts took a messy first draft and provided essential and extensive feedback through the developmental editing process. I am deeply grateful for her insights and help in tightening up the tone, themes, and language. Leonora Bulbeck performed the copy edit, which further polished a rough-hewn manuscript into the shining novel you now hold in your hands. Without her watchful eye, there would be many more missing words and spelling erors.

Of course, someone also has to make sure the book is actually readable, and that job falls to the beta readers. I have Tori Partridge, Cat Skinner, and Erin Henschel to thank for reading the text in various stages of completion and offering their kind and thoughtful feedback.

Since you've made it to the acknowledgements section, you probably judged this book worthy of your time by its beautiful cover, which was painted by the incomparable Aleksandra Wojcik. And while you made your way through the past few hundred pages, you've also been appreciating Laura Boyle's keen eye for style and typography. In the back, you'll find Auey Santos doing her best to make me look somewhat photogenic—no mean feat to say the least.

I'd like to thank Chris Baty for inspiring me to start down the path to writing a novel, and the Mechanics' Institute for giving me a quiet place to hole up and write more or less without distraction. Thanks to Thomas, Kathleen, and Kristen for their unwavering love and support.

And lastly, thank you. A book is nothing without its reader, and I hope this book was as fun for you to read as it was for me to write.